Chess with My Grandfather

Chess with My Grandfather
(A War Novel)

ARIEL MAGNUS

Translated by Kit Maude

LONDON NEW YORK CALCUTTA

This work is published within the framework of 'Sur' Translation Support Programme of the Ministry of Foreign Affairs, International Trade and Worship of the Argentine Republic.

Seagull Books, 2021

Originally published in Spanish as *El Que Mueve Las Piezas*
© Ariel Magnus, 2021
Published by arrangement with Literary Agency Michael Gaeb

First published in English translation by Seagull Books, 2021
English translation © Kit Maude, 2021

ISBN 978 0 8574 2 795 3

British Library Cataloguing-in-Publication Data
A catalogue record for this book is available from the British Library.

Typeset by Seagull Books, Calcutta, India
Printed and bound by Versa Press, East Peoria, Illinois, USA

For my grandfather
With my grandfather

There is no truer history than the novel

Miguel de Unamuno

Novel of Don Sandalio, Chess Player

CONTENTS

DISCLAIMER

This novel is a work of fiction. Full stop. And yet, many of the characters have been deliberately taken from reality and the reality of literary fiction. Any similarities to our world (or worlds) aren't really a coincidence. To keep confusion down to strictly unnecessary levels, it is beholden upon us to clarify the following:

Heinz Magnus was the actual name of the grandfather of the author of this novel. His grandson never met him, but he did genuinely find a private diary (which Heinz's children hadn't bothered to read!) and the quotes from it are faithful (as far as the translations allow).

Furthermore, a world chess championship really did take place in 1939, in the real city of Buenos Aires, and a world war really did break out during it, bringing with it real tragedy. Some of these events are described here, even if the anecdotes sound— as they say so enticingly—stranger than fiction. The chess players mentioned in this work of fiction are also real, especially the inimitable Sonja Graf, the author of the books cited in the text in *dutifully italicized passages* so as not to create confusion, or rather to encourage it when appropriate.

There's no real need (other than a mischievous urge to muddy the waters) to clarify that the writers mentioned in this book also existed, especially Ezequiel Martínez Estrada whose wonderful treatise on chess is available to the curious reader, if said curiosity has been piqued by the quotes in this book. Last but not least, it is very true that *Chess Story* by Stefan Zweig features a fictional character called Mirko Czentovic, but we know nothing about his life outside of said novel.

Everyone (the chess players, writers and even good old Grandpa Magnus) should be regarded here as fictitious characters at the mercy of the author's whims.

To put it in technical terms: 'When real historical events or real public figures, facts, places and dialogues involving them appear, they are completely imaginary and do not seek to describe actual events or to alter the fictional nature of the novel.' (I wonder whether that statement is itself subject to copyright?)

Literary litigants, widows and widowers of writers buried fewer than seventy years ago, editors who fear for the legality of the books they publish and readers who want to know exactly when to suspend and restore their disbelief have thus been forewarned.

Right, now that we've agreed on the rules, the time has come to drive you crazy with the age-old but forever young and playful skirmish of literature.

1

IF A CHARACTER HEADS THIS WAY

On the great passenger steamer due to depart New York for Buenos Aires at midnight, there was the usual last-minute bustle and commotion. Visitors from shore shoved confusedly to see off their friends, telegraph boys in cocked caps dashed through the lounges shouting names, trunks and flowers were carried past, and inquisitive children ran up and down the companionways, the orchestra playing imperturbably on deck all the while. As I was standing a bit apart from the hubbub, talking on the promenade deck with an acquaintance of mine, two or three flashbulbs flared near us—apparently the press had been quickly interviewing and photographing some celebrity just before we sailed. My friend glanced over and smiled. 'That's a rare bird you've got on board—that's Czentovich.' I must have received this news with a rather blank look, for he went on to explain, 'Mirko Czentovich, the world chess champion. He's crisscrossed America from coast to coast playing tournaments and is now off to Argentina for fresh triumphs.'

Thus begins not this novel but *Chess Story* by Stefan Zweig. It's a hard and fast rule of the game that once one has touched a piece, said piece must be moved. On the board that every player keeps forever ready in their mind, you can move your pieces backward and forward as much as you like, and even those of your opponent. In fact, this is advisable if you want to anticipate how they're going to respond to your moves. But once you've decided what move to make and your brain has sent these instructions to your arm, there's no turning back. Our brain may be a queen but our body is nothing but a pawn.

For a professional player, the irreversibility of the physical movement begins even before their fingertips have met the head of the piece: a sudden withdrawal might indicate hesitation, or even fear. And in chess, as in war, showing weakness only serves to strengthen the enemy. It's one thing to ponder a move, even for a suspiciously lengthy amount of time, and something very different to second-guess yourself, especially when you've had plenty of time to think it over. Suddenly, quiet reflection becomes uncertainty. Hesitancy is always defensive, only thought is offensive, and this game is all about attack.

More extreme thinkers suggest that the art of deciding a move begins even earlier, with the opponent's move, which in turn begins with your previous move and so on back to the beginning. So, logically, the game could well be decided by the very first move. 'After d4, White's game is up,' said one theoretician from the so-called ultramodern school. And because once it's begun not even that theoretical movement can be stopped, the Persian poet Omar Khayyam expanded upon the theory to include real life: before a player moves their piece, God moves the player. Finally (we need to stop somewhere, that's another hard and fast rule of the game. Of thought too), the poet Jorge Luis Borges continued the backward momentum ad infinitum:

> *God moves the player and he, the piece.*
> *What god behind God begins the plot*
> *of dust and time and dream and agonies*?

Getting back to the basic rule and applying it to that other game: literature, especially literature about 'The Game of Kings', it becomes clear that if Stefan Zweig wrote in *Chess Story* that the young prodigy Mirko Czentovic took a steamer from New York to Buenos Aires to take part in a tournament, the piece had been touched and we must assume that the move was completed.

When exactly this occurred is not revealed to us by the narrator but it's easy enough to work out. On the one hand, the enigmatic Dr B who appears in the novel is an Austrian arrested by the Gestapo after the Anschluss. So it had to be after March 1938. He spent several months locked up in a hotel room during which time he memorized so many chess matches that he ended up 'poisoned' by the game, says Zweig. After a brief hospital stay, he escaped to the United States, and went from there to Rio de Janeiro. Meanwhile—in both time and space—we know that Zweig wrote the book after he got to Brazil and that he arrived there in 1940 after giving a series of talks in Argentina and Paraguay. We also know that he wrote it before turning to his autobiography in 1941. *The World of Yesterday* was published after his suicide, like *Chess Story*.

So, sometime in-between Dr B's flight in the novel and the writing of said novel, the eighth Tournament of Nations was held in Buenos Aires, featuring world-famous chess players such as

Alexander Alekhine and José Raúl Capablanca among whose august company Zweig places his character. Capablanca sailed to Argentina on the Neptune, which left from Naples, and Alekhine on the Alcántara, which came from Rio de Janeiro, but the delegations from Canada and Norway came from New York on a boat bearing the rather on-the-nose name of *Argentina*. We can thus deduce with complete certainty (or show of it at least) that Mirko Czentovic also arrived on 16 August 1939, a week before the chess Olympiad of that year; the first to be held outside Europe.

And yet, this hypothesis is contradicted by an incontrovertible fact: in the database published by the Centre for Latin American Migration Studies (CEMLA), the name Mirko Czentovic does not appear under that date (or any other). Then again, neither does the name of my grandfather, Heinz Magnus, even though he arrived shortly beforehand and he was as real as I am.

2

AND ACCORDING TO THE OFFICIAL RECORDS, MY GRANDFATHER NEVER ARRIVED

13th June 1937

Eleven o'clock at night, on board the Vigo. *The monstrous ordeal is behind me; and even though deep down I feel a certain satisfaction at my success, I can't stop thinking of my parents and can only hope that things work out for them too. It's better when one keeps their expectations under control. The* Vigo. *From the outside, the ship might not look particularly grand but it has a certain dignity nevertheless. We cast off from the loading docks. People we knew waved us off affectionately; our neighbours, mostly. They'd come to wish the little boy and the gentle-man, the man who was born there, whom they'd known since he was a little boy, luck in his new homeland. They were amazed at his being forced to leave and there was sadness in their waving but also happiness; a reflection of their hope that things would go better on the other side. They kept on rhythmically waving and waving before gradually drifting away as the little ship disappeared from sight.*

The Vigo *is surprisingly clean and tidy. Tables with white tablecloths, beds with white sheets. The stewards are friendly and helpful. From the moment I embarked, I have felt the wonderfully welcoming sensation of being at home. There are a large number of visitors, so the dining room is noisy. Passengers are allowed to eat here while visitors . . . well, they get their bread too. The farewell wasn't too painful. Father and Mother will be following on soon; you'll have to make your own luck. A woman with a husband and children appears to have left a lot of happiness behind. Maybe it was the exhausting wait, the difficult bureaucracy, uncertainty about the future or her sense of responsibility that made her tears flow so. She can't seem to calm herself down. So many fates are thrown together in the melting pot of life: think of all the happiness and despair that must have been felt by those now getting ready to share three or four weeks together. The departure for South America has become a reality. Early tomorrow morning, we'll be on the open sea.*

The climate has improved greatly, the rain briefly relinquished its stranglehold on Hamburg and the sun shone down on us. By nightfall, countless dots began to appear everywhere you looked; twinkling specks sketching an outline of the city. It's completely dark now and the fairy-tale castle is complete: the port of Hamburg thrillingly defined by lights. Red and white, big and small, bright and weak, they're all part of that world, and the word seems apt; it is a world unto itself.

I know now that I am alone. I look to the sky and there's that feeling again: if God is with me, what could possibly go wrong? And so the distance ahead of us seems short: we are still on the same earth and God is the same. I haven't changed. It's good to be able to entrust myself to the embrace of God. And if he chooses me to announce his coming to men, or even simply to follow his teachings . . . why not? Perhaps after all I shall be able to perform what appears to me to be my duty to the Creator . . . I just need a little help.

This wasn't taken from a book but the private diary of my paternal grandfather Heinz Magnus, originally from Hamburg, Germany, who arrived at Dock Four, Section Eight, of the port of Buenos Aires at 7.30 on the morning of Saturday, 14th August 1937. I know that he arrived on that day because the *Vigo*'s arrival was reported in the newspapers and I know that he was on that ship because I have his private diary, whatever the CEMLA database might have to say about it (it does, however, record the arrival of my grandmother Liselotte Jacoby, who'd disembarked a few months before Mirko Czentovich).

My grandfather's diary begins earlier, in December 1935, but this is the first literary entry, or at least the first that makes an effort with the descriptions and recounts things that happened a few hours before, as one might expect from a novel told in the first person (Stefan Zweig's, for instance). The image of the lights of the port as shorthand for the far-off world to which he would never return (for the only other long-distance journey he would venture on, he chose the United States. No one in the family ever found out why, so it's up to me) might easily have appeared in one of the poems that Heinz had been writing since he was fifteen, which he collected in a notebook with a prologue and contents page that has also come into my possession. Some of these poems are striking, especially the way they anticipated the rise of the Nazis. In May 1933, a few months before Hitler came to power, my grandfather was writing a poem in German entitled 'To the Germans' that went something like this:

> *The only true tragedy*
> *Is the one seen coming from the start.*
> *For those who live it in the flesh*
> *It isn't tragedy, but destiny.*

At the tender age of nineteen, Heinz Magnus immediately saw that 'a stupidity has settled / on the minds of the masses' and that 'what is foretold cannot be undone'. A few months later, amid the violence that had started to break out in his native city, he wrote another poem entitled 'Jew!' in which he announced that belonging to the 'chosen people' compelled him to 'fulfil my obligation', the same one to which he appears to refer on the *Vigo*. In spite of this, and the fact that my family had always said that my grandfather wanted to be a rabbi, his diaries reveal that he actually wanted to be a writer.

> *It's very strange: even though I've never written before,*
> *with the exception of brief, insignificant texts, I yearn to*
> *write, to express my thoughts. So often I think about*
> *everything and feel that I too have something important*
> *to say*!

But the events of his life didn't leave him enough time for literature. First, he had to organize his and his parents' flight from Germany, then to start from scratch in Argentina and achieve a certain level of economic prosperity with his business (the watershed moment in this regard would be his trip to the United States in September and October 1950, when my grandmother was heavily pregnant with my father). After that, his heart began to fail and he died from his fourth heart attack at the age of fifty-two. My father was a teenager at the time and I wouldn't be born for another decade. Except for a couple of photos and his library, from which I have stolen books since I was a child, I never knew my grandfather until I found his diary and other papers.

It happened entirely by chance. Flipping through one of the books from the library I inherited, a little piece of paper fell out. When I folded it open, it turned out to be the instruction sheet for a medication called Cenestal, which described itself as a 'psycho-stabilizer' that 'modulates, eases and makes more real an individual's adjustment to the demands and impositions of everyday life.' As I subsequently found out, it was a psychotropic drug, one of the first to be manufactured in the country; the fact that the laboratory responsible was founded by Germans lent it an enhanced aura of reliability. Their bestselling branded drug was Dicarboxin, whose magical ingredient—piperazine—has a lot of undesirable side effects. Cenestal contained ergotamine, which today is banned in the United States and is particularly dangerous for those with heart conditions.

At a family dinner, I asked if anyone knew that Grandpa was taking the drug. That was when one of my aunts mentioned the diary, as proof that he'd always suffered from depression. But that was only the first notebook, which went up to 1940, when he met my grandmother. Going through her things, I found two more notebooks, which continue, with significant gaps, up to 1955 (the trip to the United States is covered in letters). His wife and children had kept them the way atheists keep up religious traditions, with a deep respect concealing an even deeper indifference. No one had read them; in fact, they were barely aware of their existence. However, these notebooks written by my grandfather were 'the mirror of my life', as he describes them at one point. In short: they are the book he always wanted to write and was never able to 'partly through lack of time, but partly out of restlessness'.

> *It seems very unlikely that I shall ever write a book, or rather I am sure that it will never happen* (he wrote in his third and last notebook in December 1953). *But I believe that I understand why there must be people like me, people who, for want of a better phrase, never really finish anything worthwhile but spend their time dreaming, determined that they will work their way towards it. These people must think the same way as those greater than them who have put their ideas into words and texts. They may perform the role of mediator, which is just as necessary as anything else in the world. In this regard, there is no hierarchy, there is no higher or lower, everything is on the same plane: the finite in opposition to the infinite . . .*

My grandfather's literary idol was Stefan Zweig. There was even a rumour in my family that they were related because my grandfather's mother's maiden name was Zweig. I found my mother's birth certificate among my grandfather's papers and her father (i.e. my great-grandfather) was indeed called Hans Zweig and was from Eisleben, Martin Luther's home town. We were Zweigs but not a branch of Stefan Zweig's Austrian family: we belonged to Arnold Zweig's Polish one. Arnold was also a Jewish writer, but he was German. According to my eldest aunt, there was a connection with the Zweigs along both family branches ('Zweig' actually means branch in German). And yet there is no evidence that Stefan and Arnold were related, unless the Magnus branch is the missing link.

Proof of my grandfather's admiration for his apocryphal relative can be found in the address book he used to keep a record of the books he bought and read. Under the letter Z, fifteen books by Stefan Zweig are listed, more than any other author in the library. The same enthusiasm can be seen in his reading log, which generally contained little more than summaries of the books with few personal opinions. 'To read books, to read more and more books, that is what one wants to do whenever one finishes a Zweig,' he says in his diary after *The World of Yesterday*. And in the log entry for *Beware of Pity*, he writes: 'A masterpiece, extraordinarily gripping and full of wonderful knowledge.' The latter was a gift from my grandmother for his first birthday after they had started going out, which seems to me the clearest evidence available of how much my grandfather revered the author.

I'd like to say that the latter book has a label from the bookshop Pigmalión in addition to the *ex libris* bookplate inscribed with the name Enrique Magnus, as he was known in Argentina. But there are no stamps or labels, and as the dedication from my grandmother is dated 1941, she couldn't possibly have bought it from a bookshop that opened the following year. Other books I inherited from him do have the black sticker and flowery lettering from the celebrated bookshop at 515 Calle Corrientes, which specialized in books in German and other foreign languages. Owned by another German Jew in exile, Lili Lebach, Pigmalión (my favourite myth, by the way) became famous because it was frequented by Jorge Luis Borges and also because it published the first edition of *Chess Story*, not in translation but in the original language, earlier than Zweig's regular publishers in Stockholm and London. It was the first and only book to be published by the bookshop in a special edition of 250 numbered copies.

I am certain that my grandfather bought that edition. The book appears in his log before others by Zweig that he bought in subsequent years. But it wasn't in his library. It's a pity, not just because of the lost thrill of owning something that almost directly connects me to Stefan Zweig (the edition was based on the manuscript he sent to his Spanish translator, which has disappeared) but most of all because my grandfather used to keep things in his books, everything from newspaper clippings to, as we've seen, instructions for medicines (never any money though, Grandpa!) and it might have helped me resolve a great mystery about his life.

I have my suspicions about where that book ended up. As a numbered first edition, it must have been quite valuable. An internet search for my grandfather's name turned up a 2001 exhibition of Jewish children's books in Frankfurt, among which was an unusual *ex libris* bookplate signed by one Enrique Magnus.

The exhibition description reads:

> *A book swims from one continent to another. This* ex libris *signed by Enrique Magnus, who was probably known as Heinz Magnus before his emigration, symbolizes the fate of the 420 pieces shown in the exhibition 'The Lives of Jewish Children as Seen in Their Books'.*

I wrote an email to the museum asking when they'd bought the book and from whom because I don't believe that my grandfather ever sold any that belonged to him. In their answer, they said that they'd bought the book for the bookplate. The ostentatious, oversized illustration of a book floating across the Atlantic Ocean between the Americas and Europe is a little different from the traditional kind of *ex libris*, both for the dramatic image it conjures and its relatively poor quality. To show you what I mean, the easiest thing would be to reproduce an image of said bookplate but this is a Jewish novel, at least in the sense that it adheres to the second Commandment: thou shalt not worship graven images. Thence, perhaps, our secret yearning for Pygmalion's Galatea.

The museum's reply also gave me the name of the bookseller who sold them the bookplate, who turned out to be the grandfather of a school friend of mine. The business of the man whom I would never meet consisted of buying whole libraries cheaply, especially within the German Jewish community, from which he would only sell on a couple of books, albeit for sizeable sums to wealthy buyers. From Europe, in this case. My hypothesis is that he must have bought the children's book along with the rest of the library of someone who knew my grandfather, or who at least had his book, perhaps along with many others.

As is generally the case, my grandfather had *ex libris* labels made up because he often loaned out books that weren't returned. Ironically, as it turned out, it was the label that was supposed to ensure the book's return that became the main reason that it wasn't. But I think that he still would have been proud that something he had created ended up being more valuable than the book itself, which was even placed on display in a museum in the country of his birth. The effort he put into its composition shows that he was using the excuse of wanting to protect his books as a means of making his mark on them, in the most Pygmalianesque, artistic sense of the term. But it's a shame for me because it has probably deprived me of being able to quote from a first edition of *Chess Story* and perhaps even finding among its pages more information about Mirko Czentovich's time in Buenos Aires.

I do, in contrast, know something about what Stefan Zweig was doing in Buenos Aires. He visited the city in 1940 before moving on to Brazil. Let me quote again from the diary:

29th October 1940

Today I went to listen to Stefan Zweig talk about 'The unity of the spirit in the world'. A lecture in Spanish at the Free College. The essence of the talk was that borders between nations and people are unnatural, we are all fully capable of understanding one another. He made a particularly fine comparison to music, explaining that everyone can understand it and that it conveys something to everyone in a universal language. Then he argued that the spirit of culture could no longer be based in Europe so he called on those of us over here to be the heirs of its great cultural patrimony. I was expecting much more from the talk but I couldn't help notice that even at that rather basic level he didn't seem to be making much of an impression on the locals.

It was then that I realized in shock that our wonderful culture, which had been so carefully cherished in Europe, would be lost forever if it didn't find people to continue to protect and nurture it. North America isn't the right place for the culture in question. We will lose it, it will certainly slip away from us if a group of people don't get together to save what they can. And so I have given myself the mission, so long as I have the time and financial resources available, to try to gather together by early next winter some people to bring this about. Now we must think clearly about how this might be done. Suddenly, I have discovered a truly mighty task for myself.

Germany had invaded France and my grandfather was convinced that a Nazi triumph would mean a return to the 'darkest of dark ages', which is why he was so determined to preserve what was left. An entry the following year mentions the mission again in the same nigh-on delirious, megalomaniac tone demonstrating, by the way, that my grandfather wasn't depressive but if anything manic depressive, the contemporary term for which is bipolar. The treatment for said condition is psychotropic drugs.

3rd April 1941

*There is a sentence in 'Disraeli' that speaks of Caesar or Napoleon—*he writes in English—*Imagine had they died unrecognized, always conscious that their supernatural energies might die away without creating their miracles. Sometimes I would think something very near to it. Now although very seldom I get this supernatural feeling of being destined for a special mission. But the less I follow the way of God the less this feeling is produced.*

When he had boarded the *Vigo* five years earlier, Magnus saw the mission he envisaged for himself as having been given to him by God. God's place would then be taken by Stefan Zweig. This explains why, in the red leatherette portfolio containing his documents and other important papers that also came into my possession, he kept a clipping from the newspaper *Crítica* showing a photograph of the writer and his wife lying dead in their bed in Petrópolis. Zweig's suicide in early 1942 came as a harsh blow to my grandfather. In a letter he wrote to his best friend, which was so important to him that he stuck a copy into his diary, he shares his pain:

> *There is a great pain in my heart. I keep having to remind myself: Stefan Zweig is dead, Stefan Zweig is dead. Inconceivable, unsayable . . .*

Then Magnus provides an account of the talk in 1940, and describes the writer as seeming worn out and defeated. Without trying to justify it, he saw the suicide as a liberating act: Zweig's heart, overwhelmed by a common feeling with so many others, couldn't stand the sadness and desperation of the world. 'I am devoted to Zweig,' he says in the same letter which ends with the announcement that on Sunday he would be reading a new novella by Zweig along with his soon-to-be wife Liselotte Jacoby.

And so Magnus kept those horrible 'photos exclusive to *Crítica* brought by plane' next to vital documents such as his savings book and the cards from the Jewish cemetery in Tablada marking where his parents were buried. And it is only this context that explains my surprise at finding among his papers a certificate from 1956 stating that my grandfather was actually a Catholic:

> *Monsignor Dr Alejandro Schell, Prelate of His Holiness, Church of our Lady of Peace, certifies that Enrique Magnus, originally from Germany and a naturalized Argentine for the past twenty years, currently living on Monroe 4140, Capital Federal, is an Apostolic Roman Catholic and is 42 years old.*

As someone who has known him for some time, I hereby confirm that the above is true and incontestable.

The newspaper clipping next to the one about Zweig's death is a long column from a 1963 edition of *La Nación* newspaper announcing that said Monsignor Alejandro Schell was appointed by the Pope to be Bishop of the Diocese of Lomas de Zamora. What might have interested my grandfather about the posting of a Monsignor? How did he know him, and why did he issue that false certificate? Why did he want said certificate?

Unlike the discovery of the Cenestal instructions, no one in the family was able to shed any light on this second piece of paper. One possibility is that it might be related to his heart condition: he went to see several doctors including one Dr Tiburcio Padilla, who ran the Hospital de Clínicas. It was rumoured that Padilla was anti-Semitic because when he was Minister of Public Health for the military government that overthrew the Frondizi administration, he took over the Malbrán Institute and fired its director, Ignacio Pirosky. The new director got rid of four members of the molecular biology division which was carrying out very advanced genetic research for the time. The head of that division was another Jew, César Milstein, who immediately resigned and went to Cambridge where he would later win the Nobel Prize in Medicine. In another article from 1963, I read that according Dr Tiburcio Padilla 'psychiatric wards should be installed in every national and municipal hospital to dispel the myth that all crazy people think they're Napoleon (the phrase is Alberto Mondet's); it's just another disease, like a liver or heart condition, or tuberculosis.'

Did Padilla hate Jews so much that he refused to treat them? Did my grandfather have the certificate made up to fool him? Was it he who prescribed the deadly Cenestal in the late '50s, just before my grandfather's first heart attack, in the belief that bipolarity is a disease that one cures with drugs rather than therapy?

These questions, to which one is unlikely to find answers through documentary research, were what inspired me to write this novel, but it also belongs to my grandfather. I am convinced that the beginning to the mystery must be sought in the chess tournament of 1939 and the book that Heinz Magnus was never able to write for lack of time (and an excess of restlessness). Evidence that fiction ran through his veins can be seen not only in his diary entry about the *Vigo*, but also in the only story that ever made it all the way to me, suggestively titled 'The Discovery':

It was a spring morning, a real spring morning. Although the sun shone in a blue sky dotted with little white clouds, winter's chill still clung to the air. She appeared in the doorway. The young girl led her that far, gave her her rubber-bottomed cane and quickly disappeared back into the dark hallway. The old lady looked to be about sixty years of age even though she was well past her seventieth birthday. The youthful sheen on an almost wrinkle-free face was accentuated by the deep black of her hair, strands of which stuck out in different directions from beneath her hat. She appeared to have difficulty walking; after a few quick steady but uneven steps, she would stop to rest on her cane. This stuttering motion was how she got about. The path led to the largest park in the city, which was excellently located. Some of the benches, placed next to clusters of trees and bushes, looked enormously inviting. The old woman sat down on one. Children passed by, jumping around and laughing at their game, their parents following with amused expressions while other visitors had their cameras capture the essence of nature within their dark contraptions. After a brief rest, the old woman stood back up and went on a little way before freezing suddenly. She hadn't got far enough in her routine for another pause. Something out of the ordinary must have happened to stop the grande dame in her tracks.

She looked down at the ground, then again, more closely than before, blinking uncertainly, as though she couldn't quite see. Then she lifted her cane, poked the earth a little and bent forward. She wasn't entirely sure if it was what she thought it was. She pawed at the object a little with her foot to lift it out of the sand and pebbles.

'Oh yes, it's a 50-pfennig coin,' she said to herself.

She tried to bend down but stood back up again immediately. Then she repeated the movement but couldn't get all the way down with her cane. So she stood back up again, held the cane out horizontally in one hand, bent down lower and lower, knees buckling, put the hand holding the cane on the ground and picked up the coin with her free hand. Then she lurched back up, gasping in relief. She inspected the coin. She was stunned. Her face crumpled into a frown, revealing hidden wrinkles. She threw her new 50-pfennig coin into the sand. She'd been holding a coin that had been withdrawn from circulation. After carefully dusting herself off, she continued on her way. Soon her face lit up, the wrinkles disappeared and a little smile tugged at each side of her mouth as she thought about the inscription on the out of date coin: 'God helps those who help themselves.'

3

TO FORCE A MATCH

Like Mirko Czentovic, Sonja Graf came to the country by her own means and wasn't certain of her place in the tournament. When the Nazis came to power, she moved into exile in London where she contrived to play under whatever flag she could find against Vera Menchik de Stevenson, the reigning women's champion.

And it was with her that she was walking through the only overseas branch of Harrods that ever existed. The department store was celebrating the end of its financial year with a 'Grand pre-inventory sale' that promised 'genuinely sacrificial' (!) prices. Although neither of the chess players was especially interested in purchasing a cut-price set of British crockery, they were amazed that such a building, which would have stood out even in London and contained luxury items that one couldn't even get in Berlin, could be found in this remote, oddly southerly city. In fact, everything in Buenos Aires, beginning with the cold, felt out of place. In addition to providing protection from the genuinely wintery temperatures outside, walking indoors had another advantage. Before embarking for Argentina, Graf had heard that it was a country populated by semi-savage Indians unfamiliar with basic conveniences such as cars. Once she'd got off the boat, however, she found that in fact the greatest hazard in the city wasn't indigenous tribes but the very cars that weren't supposed to be there, although they did drive on the left-hand side, just like in London. *'The people crossing the streets, doing pirouettes in-between the thousands of automobiles was a novelty that brought me joy and anxiety in equal measure. One expected an accident at every turn,'* she'd write later in *This is How a Woman Plays*, one of the two books she'd publish after moving to the country.

'No, not my father, my friend's father!' Sonja was saying at that exact moment as she hopped down from the stairs.

'What friend?' Vera was following her slowly, at an elephantine pace, remembering the mechanical escalator in the Harrods in London with fondness and wondering which was really more of a luxury: marble or technology.

'The one I told you about, who invited me home because it was too late to go back to mine.'

Between her faltering English and the distraction of her colleague, Graf's spontaneous confession ran serious risk of being misinterpreted (which is exactly what happened, judging by the references to the abuse she suffered as a child that circulate in magazines and on the internet). She wasn't a victim of sexual assault at home, although she was beaten by her father and neglected by her mother. In fact, she witnessed abuse in another house, the one belonging to the friend who'd invited her to spend the night. She provides a clear account in her otherwise rather muddled autobiography *I am Susann*, the other book she would publish in Spanish, although to describe the text as such might be to stretch the truth a little: it seems to be a sotto-voce translation, so literal at times one can easily see the German lurking behind it.

There was a time when Susann—Graf uses her real name to talk about herself in the third person—*was sent by her parents every day to the home of her married sister to help take care of her children and do some domestic chores. She performed these tasks very diligently because it offered her a chance to escape from the tyranny of her parents. Generally, she returned in the afternoon.*

One day, she met a former school friend and they both started to attend dances, parties and cinemas and go out with boys. When her father asked why she had come back late the night before, Susann would say:

'I stayed at my sister's house.'

One night, when it was very late, Susann, scared, told her friend that she couldn't go home at that hour and she couldn't go to her sister's either. What should she do? Her friend suggested that she could stay in her room. She agreed! But before going inside her friend said:

'Be careful, take off your shoes and don't make any noise, I sleep in my parents' room.'

'Fine.'

They snuck in quietly and no one noticed their arrival. After a long silence, she heard the father whisper:

'Are you there, daughter? You came home very late. Aren't you cold . . . ?'

'Yes, I'm cold.'

'So, why don't you get into bed with me? I can warm you up a little.'

She got out of her bed and into her father's. About twenty minutes passed; suddenly, Susann refused to believe her ears, but father and daughter were undoubtedly having intimate relations . . .

Immense disgust crushed the heart of the guest and her throat constricted. She got up before dawn, saying goodbye without a word about what she'd seen. After that she avoided the girl and tried to forget the awful, unbelievable event.

What she witnessed, and especially what she suspected had passed unseen wasn't just a horrible shock but also had immediate consequences for her own life. Two months later, a detective came to her house and told her that he was investigating rumours of the father's incestuous behaviour. He asked her if she, as a friend, had witnessed anything out of the ordinary. Although Sonja considered lying at first, the man persisted 'skilfully, swearing that her name would never come up and that she had an obligation to God to tell him what she knew because a crime like that went against all human law.'

Susann/Sonja told him what she'd seen, and two months later she was called to testify at the trial, which was the talk of the town. At court she experienced intimidation and fear for the first time. After she was sworn in and provided an account of what she had seen, she also got her first taste of the wiles of lawyers.

Approaching Susann with a false expression of sympathy, he asked:

'And have you had anything to do with men?'

Blushing right to her ears, she answered:

'That is absolutely personal and private and I refuse to answer.'

To which he replied:

'Well! Think about it, why won't you say?'

She repeated herself very clearly:

'I refuse to answer!'

The girl could see searing malice in the eyes of her unpleasant interrogator. He spoke again:

'So, how do you know that father and daughter were having intimate relations?'

Susann . . . paralysed with despair, was found guilty of perjury while the real culprit and his daughter were declared innocent and set free. And they call that justice!

Sonja/Susann spent ten days in prison. Afterwards she was subject to physical punishment by her father. Later, she was locked away in a correctional institution run by nuns. All she would remember from the institution was a vague and pleasant, if slightly guilty, memory of a fleeting encounter with a fellow inmate in a dark stairwell. But she never said anything about that to her colleague Vera Munchik. It would only come out years later in her book, perhaps because of the unreal sheen her life took when set down in a foreign language (right now she was speaking in another: English).

The curious part, however, isn't what Graf didn't tell Menchik but the fact that she decided to share the deeply private memory of that horrible experience with someone who was little more to her than her most talented rival. Maybe it was because she never knew whether her friend had taken her home without realizing how strange her family arrangement was, or so that she would have someone with whom to share her suffering. In the absence of someone to play chess with, Sonja had been wondering about it again, and now she was pondering aloud to a fellow chess player as though her brilliant rival might help her to resolve the mystery. The most likely explanation, however, is that it was a ploy: a preliminary move, conscious or otherwise, to put her opponent off her game, a sneaky opening gambit.

Even so, her chances of winning were slim. The woman representing Russia-cum-Great Britain had been the reigning champion since the first world championship in 1927 and seemed destined to keep the title for the rest of her life. And, in fact, she would. Not in the ordinary, figurative sense of the term, for a long time, but because her life would soon be at an end. Towards the end of the war, she would be caught in the blast of one of Hitler's V2 *Wunderwaffe* rockets in London. The cruel irony of her fate was that the 'miracle' weapon was also the Nazis' star addition to Wehrschach, a form of chess they invented on a 121-square board with pieces shaped like warplanes, tanks, soldiers and the much-admired V2 rockets. The Nazis also created the first national chess association so as to exclude the Jews who were members of the regional associations, and declared Schach the 'intellectual war sport of the German people' because during the game the pieces, as the propaganda had it, 'fought to destroy the enemy' following the orders of their Führer (if they'd had read Omar Khayyam, they'd have known that it didn't end there!).

However, Sonja Graf was the first woman capable of challenging the eternal champion for her throne, and to do so she was ready to use all the weapons at her disposal, including, apparently, intimate confessions shared under the veil of professional fellowship.

And yet she didn't plan to triumph in the name of her country, whose government she detested more than her rival. She had campaigned for the right to play under another flag; her own. On the ship she thought that the most provocative move would be to adopt the one belonging to the Zionist movement seeking to create a State of Israel for its oppressed people. She liked that there was a big Star of David in the centre of its flag, almost a direct riposte to the Nazi swastika. She'd heard that one of the movement's proposals was to form the Jewish homeland somewhere in Argentina,[1] which might also perhaps explain why the flag was white and blue. But she doubted this would meet approval from the authorities, not to mention her colleagues from Palestine.

'Ruth wore a sunhat like that,' said Menchik, pointing at a mannequin's wax head sporting a shock of chestnut hair so real it could only be human.

'Ruth who?' Sonja, asked, lighting a cigarette with the butt of a previous one, as she did when she played (more proof that for her, the match had already begun!).

'Ruth Block-Nakkeruf, the Norwegian I told you about, the one the men on the ship named "Miss Chess".'

Sonja had forgotten the name out of jealousy (she hated so-called ideals of feminine beauty), but now it came as a relief. A woman who wore extravagant hats like that couldn't possibly compete with her, who always went bareheaded or, if pushed, provocatively donned a bowler hat. For similar reasons, she'd

---

1 Cf. *The Jewish State* by Theodor Herzl (1896): 'Argentina is one of the richest countries on earth, vast in size, scarce in population with a moderate climate. It would be very much in the Republic of Argentina's interests to cede us a portion of their land.'

recently adopted a side-parting along with a short haircut and, later, a tie to give her an increasingly masculine look. Other women could be feminine, including Vera Menchik with the shapeless barrel she called a body and her overfed baby face, but masculinity was a bewitching look restricted to a few. Basically just her and Marlene Dietrich. In that order, Sonja thought, because as the Miss Marlene of chess she was already the greater intellectual; another (supposedly) male characteristic.

But this combative petulance, as expressed in the way she dressed and thought, concealed her deep frustration at not having been able to shine among men in chess-playing terms. Although she'd beaten or drawn with a few famous players such as Rudolf Spielmann and Paul Keres, this had been during simultaneous games or at minor competitions. Competing and giving them a royal beating had been her dream ever since her father had forbidden her from going to the Munich Chess Club with her brothers, scandalized by the mere idea of a young lady entering such an environment. And neither did professional chess players like the idea of the fairer sex seeing the game as anything more than a pastime. It was said, for example, that the Austrian Albert Becker had declared that anyone who lost against a woman should suffer the indignity of joining a club bearing said woman's name. In 1929, Becker faced Vera Menchik de Stevenson and became the first member of her club. He would be joined by other stars of the chess-playing firmament, giving Menchik the aura of a mortal allowed to compete with and even humiliate the gods. In that sense, she had been far more successful at beating men at their own game, and no amount of cross-dressing could close the gap.

Sonja went on ahead to the area where the music was coming from and started to inspect the tango records, the only one of the country's exports she was familiar with other than beef (although she thought that the former sounded Parisian and the latter also came from several other neighbouring countries). Though Carlos Gardel had got himself killed a few years before and although she didn't know his name then, the voice coming from the gramophone sounded familiar somehow, as though he was singing in French.

And she also was able to follow the lyrics, if not well, enough to know that they weren't indigenous. Strange that such bourgeois music, played on classical instruments, hadn't suggested to her that perhaps the place where it had been composed wasn't quite so backward as she'd assumed, not that she could have been expected to anticipate Buenos Aires, which was similar to Paris even in its damp chill. But she might have foreseen a little civilization (or the European idea of it anyway). Who did she think had composed this music, or invented the dance? Cows standing in a field in the Pampas? Nomadic gauchos while they slaughtered their livestock?

The music suddenly came to a halt. Sonja turned towards the gramophone and saw an important-looking man gesticulating; at least his outfit suggested he was important (everyone in this city seemed to dress well, subordinates especially), certainly more so than his demeanour. It must be one of the Harrods managers, she thought, dressing down an employee for putting on sultry, brothel music in a premises that gloried in the name 'the empire of elegance'.

The employee changed the record and now an opera was playing, featuring a woman singing in a very shrill tone. At that moment

Harry Golombeck and the rest of the British team, who she and Vera had left behind a little while ago, appeared at the other end of the hall. Sonja couldn't help repress an amused smile when she realized that the manager's intention had been to welcome the Europeans with a record, any record, recorded on their continent. She was especially irritated by the well-meaning assumption that a chess player must enjoy classical music, painting and literature when the truth was that most were accountants, or at the most musicians with no particular interest in high culture in any of its incarnations. If there was one aspect where chess could certainly be considered a sport, it was that its athletes were as philistine as boxers.

Determined to avoid being dragged back into the amiable lethargy of the 'high-tea team' by her companion's sloth (a faithful reflection of how she moved the pieces across the board), she quickly slipped off on her own, even though that meant leaving behind her rival and with it the chance to continue her gambit. Deep down she knew that it was absurd to think that anything she might say before they faced off might influence the result, but she also sensed (rightly) that this, the second occasion on which they'd competed for the title, would be the definitive one, so only a fool would fail to do everything they could to tip the balance in their favour. Two years ago, she had lost 2–9, a proportionally worse result than that at an exhibition tournament in 1930 when she'd been defeated 1–3. Allowing things to take their natural course could only make things worse. In fact, on closer inspection, the progression meant that she wasn't even technically qualified to participate in the tournament, so the game within the game had actually begun a few weeks before when she'd taken the bulky packet boat headed for Buenos Aires.

With these thoughts in mind, most pressingly that she needed
to make sure that she had a place in the competition, Sonja got
onto a lift. She wanted to visit the tea-room on the eighth floor
before she left, not so much for its awe-inspiring decor or the supposed pedigree of its clientele but for the sweets available there,
her great indulgence other than tobacco and alcohol. The lift, contrary to its name, didn't lead up to the terrace but down to the
basement (and even though its German name is 'travel chair', you
still have to stand up in them). She waited for the iron cage to
begin its etymologically correct journey back upwards but the
operator took so long to begin the return journey that she eventually decided to get out and visit what appeared to be an instal-
lation of Roman baths—a well-lit space clad in Carrara marble.
It turned out to be a beauty salon.

There were separate areas for ladies and gentlemen. She naturally headed for the latter and was just as naturally accepted as
such. She was led to a table where she could wait for one of the
occupied chairs to open up (a haircut and shave for 75 cents!)
Attracted less by the discount than the opportunity to rest her
feet and in the process take in the unedifying spectacle of men
grooming other men like monkeys picking the bugs off their
babies, Graf sat down next to a man with wavy hair and a serious
bearing. The young man, keen on taking the chance to be attended
in such a distinguished venue on the cheap, was doodling in the
margins of a newspaper full of photographs. In one of them, Graf
saw Menchik standing on the deck of the ocean liner next to an
ongoing interview. She thought rather bitterly that no one had
been waiting to interview her when she arrived; she had had to
seek out one of the journalists from *La Razón* who just happened
to be wandering around the port. He had published a photo of

her in which the focus was very much on her legs (she had arrived during a winter heat wave when temperatures had reached 18 degrees Celsius, unleashing an epidemic of shingles). The summery photograph was accompanied by a brief, unpleasant caption that fortunately, being unfamiliar with Spanish, Graf couldn't read:

Sonja Graf is a relaxed, talkative woman, not at all feminine or handsome but pleasant and friendly. She is well aware of this, remarking to us on the dock that 'one doesn't have to be pretty to play chess well.'

Getting back to the young man with the thinning hair, what he was apparently trying to set down on paper was a sketch of half the planet spanning Europe and Argentina but it looked as though he was as ignorant of geography as Columbus or any of the other cartographers who were either misled by inaccurate reports or simply made things up as they saw fit.

'Shit!' he said in German.

'You speak German!' Sonja exclaimed in surprise.

'A woman!' the German exclaimed back.

'And why not?'

'For no reason that I can think of. But you'll miss out on your shave.'

Sonja smiled. She enjoyed the company of men because as serious as they might seem on the outside, deep down they always tended to be funny. And cocky. Everything that women apparently weren't supposed to be.

'Well, whenever I went to the circus, I wanted to be the bearded lady. You?'

Now it was the young gentleman's turn to smile. No one had ever asked him a question like that. He thought of his mission on earth, his relationship with God, the meaning of life. In his diary he asked questions like:

The Earth dies, man dies, but is that reason to despair? If material things can seem so essential, is it even possible to gauge the worth of the world of the spirit?

Or:

Has Strauss reached Argentina? Is there music that envelops you, with which one lives? I suddenly realize how close our ties with German culture are. Beethoven, Mozart, Haydn, Mendelssohn, Strauss and so many others. Is that obvious? What will it be like on the other side? Will we occasionally feel nostalgia for the days when we enjoyed these readily available things, the times when one was able to absorb them?

Or:

Where am I? Can I still love? Doesn't life mean love? Can one live without love?

But the circus performer he'd want to be was not a question he'd ever have considered, not in a hundred years of diary entries.

'A dwarf,' he said with surprising alacrity. 'One of those dwarves that fly through the air.'

'You want to be cannon fodder? You've chosen the wrong continent!'

Sonja remembered her entrance into Harrods; instead of a tall black man dressed in white, the door had been opened by a dwarf in green livery, and added:

'Dwarves scare me.'

'Well, I'm scared of bearded ladies!'

The woman stroked her non-existent beard (she'd have loved for it to be there, for a little while at least) and made as if to light another cigarette but then stopped herself so she could continue to enjoy the scent of the lotions for men. In another fit of auto-biographical openness similar to the one she'd experienced with Vera, she was tempted to tell the boy about the time she'd worn not a beard but a moustache while she was touring Spain. Later, she would write about it in *This is How a Woman Plays*:

> *One night we attended a masked ball with the Koltanow-skis. I was wearing my men's suit and had painted a thin moustache over my lips. When I made my entrance, the women stared at me unambiguously . . . Determined to enjoy myself, I invited one of them to dance and she agreed so enthusiastically that I felt a little guilty. I continued with my 'conquests' and danced with all the women in the room until eventually, exhausted, I took refuge on the feather sofa. One of my friends, aware of my disguise, came over to ask me to dance with him. I didn't want the poor man to think that I was rejecting him so we stepped onto the dance floor.*
>
> *Imagine, my good reader, the effect this had on the women! They started to chatter and soon the mumbling reached the ears of the establishment's manager who came*

over very gruffly and said: 'I'm sorry gentlemen, but we don't allow men to dance with each other here.'

We had to accept this and, so as not to disappoint all those women, I remained a man for the entire night.

Afraid to disappoint her new companion as well, Graf stayed quiet.

'We should start our own circus,' she said instead. 'What's your name?'

'Magnus, Heinz Magnus.'

'Magnus & Graf. What do you think?'

'Graf & Magnus sounds better,' he said gallantly before adding, perhaps a little too quickly, 'Is that your married name?'

'My husband's over there.'

Sonja pointed to one of the men getting their hair cut on the large leather chairs, the ugliest of them all (she'd taken pity on him, imagine if she knew that behind those plain features lurked the best poet of the century) and the only one not gazing stupidly into the bevelled mirrors (he was already losing his sight). In that, the barber shop really did resemble a Roman bath—the men sneaked in there so they could act like women.

'No, I'm talking nonsense,' Sonja said. 'My name is Sonja and I'm single. In fact, my name is Susann. Sonja is my artistic name.'

'Do you paint?' It didn't occur to Magnus that she might be an actress, not because he didn't think it likely but because just then he needed someone who could draw.

'No. Well, probably better than you, but no, I'm a chess player.'

Magnus was confused, either by Sonja's trade, the fact that she considered it an art, or the cheeky way in which she'd made fun of his drawing, we'll never know.

'It's a symbolic drawing,' he said eventually. 'A book that travels between two continents, see?'

Sonja looked at it dubiously and asked what it was supposed to symbolize. Magnus answered proudly that it was an *ex libris* bookplate. She replied that she needed one too but in the shape of a flag.

'Something to symbolize my freedom,' she said.

'An "ex libre",' Magnus ventured, trying his hand at wordplay with unfamiliar words. The joke fell as flat as his attempts at drawing continents.

Then he turned the newspaper over and scrawled out a flag with the word 'Free' in the middle. He tore it out (he'd have rather used scissors, as he did for his newspaper clippings) and put it on the table.

'For me?' Graf asked, moved. 'How lovely. I'll use it in the tournament. Goebbels forbade me from using the German one.'

'He forbade me from living in Germany.'

Sonja glanced up from the clipping and for the first time looked at him through her real, woman's eyes. Magnus could only stand it for a few seconds, then he took off glasses that were perfectly clean and wiped them with the tip of his tie. Sonja wanted to ask if he was Jewish but instead blurted out that she was half-Gypsy. Of course he was Jewish, look at that nose. She wanted to kiss it. She wanted to embrace him in the name of all the German people who weren't on the murderers' side. Instead, she got up and said: 'Well, I have to go.'

35

'May I accompany you?' Magnus asked without getting up, worried that his legs might have turned to jelly.

'I think I can face the green dwarf at the entrance alone, and I don't want you to miss your turn.'

And she walked off, waving her freedom flag as she went but not before inviting him to come watch her play at the Politeama Theatre.

Heinz watched her go with an expression that made the other customers wonder at the morality of their relationship. Aware as we are of the disguise, what might perhaps scandalize us is that from the perspective of the twenty-six-year-old man, Miss Graf, who was over thirty, was practically an old woman. But because she wore her hair short, like my grandmother, in addition to other similarities (they were both clever and German, short but with good figures and bore dreamy, somewhat startled expressions), there are plenty of reasons to suppose that my grandfather liked her in spite of her age. Even though she wasn't Jewish, she seemed like she was, at least in the sense that she was against the Nazis. What it came down to in the end was that at the time my grandfather was searching somewhat desperately for love:

Actually, I have nothing to report—he writes on 10 September 1939, just a few days later—*but sometimes one feels the need to say something, more to express feelings than words or things. My hope is to find someone with whom I can live as good companions. Not as one, but as very good friends. I believe that the sexual aspect is certainly a part of that.*

4

A LOST CAUSE

'I don't have anything against chess,' he said, pointing to the legs of the chess player in the photograph in *La Razón*. 'My objection is that it isn't a sport. And this is the Sports Section. It's as though I were asking you to put, I don't know, a recipe in the International News Section. It could be as international a food as you like, coleslaw maybe, but it still wouldn't be appropriate. And you're trying to take half a page away from boxing, which couldn't be more different from chess. This is a fool's errand.'

This forthright speaker, who was chewing on an Imparciales cigarette (what other brand would a journalist smoke?) was J. Yanofsky, about whom we know only through an anecdote that would appear much later in a digital chess weekly:

Among the curious events that history tells us occurred at the Olympiad, the following anecdote stands out: two brothers of the surname Yanofksy met there for the first time, each playing for a different country. J. Yanofsky, 45, was born in the Ukraine and left for Argentina in 1919. His father stayed in the Ukraine and later emigrated to Canada, taking his six-month-old son Abe Yanofsky with him. Abe grew up to become the best chess player in Canada and was named to play as first board. Having seen the list of participants, J. Yanofksy was surprised and anxious to meet A. Yanofsky from the Canadian team. When he showed a photo of his father to Abe, the latter exclaimed: 'That's my father too!' and they joyfully embraced.

What the source calls 'history' is little more than an anonymous comment on a web page dedicated to Daniel Abraham (Abe) Yanofsky. The other Yanofksy isn't listed among the members of the Argentinian or any other team. Abe Yanofsky himself leads us to question its veracity: in his account of the tournament in the memoir *Chess the Hard Way!* he makes no mention of an event that deserves a book unto itself. So was it made up, like Mirko Czentovich? Almost. The *La Razón* of Saturday, 26th August, contains the following:

The kid Yanofksy looks stunned. And with good reason. He's found his brother in Buenos Aires and is playing the Tournament of Nations for the first time. This is now a family affair.

The section that records this anecdote for posterity is called 'Among the Boards' and is signed by 'Public Spectator Number 1'. It features entries such as: 'He believed in democracy: he tried out the French defence.' And 'Some of the participants' surnames try one's patience. They're like an alphabet in reverse.' As you can see, it was a humorous section, or tried to be. It wouldn't be beyond the bounds of belief to suspect that the Yanofsky anecdote was an in-joke between colleagues that we (the royal we, dear Grandpa) shall now continue, once again obliged by the touch-move rule, in this tournament of (literary) notions, journalism providing the missing link between reality and fiction.

'Instead of staring at the German girl's legs, look: here are the registrations for the chess tournament and right next door you have the photo of the Argentinian after being hit below the belt by the Chilean.'

We shall call the editor of the International Section Renzi, like Ricardo Piglia's alter ego, the journalist from *Artificial Respiration*. Given the year, however, he'd have to be his father or, better yet, grandfather. The editor of the International Section, Emilio Renzi (the grandfather) was bent over the copy of the newspaper where Yanofsky had worked before moving on to *Crítica*. A few minutes earlier, he'd tried to convince him of the similarities between the two sports, bringing up an article in which an Argentinian chess player said that, as preparation for the world championship, he'd taken boxing classes, and that the first thing he did when he got to the 'concentration camp' (which you could still call training camps in 1939) was to ask if there was a punching bag.

'Dirty Chilean!' Yanofsky didn't even look at the article; he'd been at the fight. 'He was messing with our guy right from the first round. If it wasn't a head butt, it was a push or some other shitty move. See? You can't do that in chess. And it's a part of the sport. If pushed, I'd say it was the most important part.'

He angrily stubbed out his cigarette as though he were still at the ring. Well, the ashtray was ring-shaped.

'So you approve of the Chilean's cheating, even though he lost?' Renzi asked. 'That makes no sense.'

'It makes sporting sense, Emilio. It sounds simple but it's more complicated than chess.'

Renzi asked him to explain himself and Yanofsky politely declined; his argument was riddled with contradictions. Renzi countered that chess had its own murky areas. And he wasn't referring to the pieces: in fact, they hadn't always been black and white even if the 'chessboard' pattern was now sacrosanct, as though God had created it along with leopards ('leopard print', he felt the need to add). When chess was first invented, there were only white squares: only when it got to the West did a second colour get added, to make things clearer.

Yanofsky puffed out his cheeks in admiration, lit another cigarette and asked Renzi why he wasn't covering the tournament in the International Section if he knew so much about it. Most of the participants were foreigners after all, he said amid a billow of smoke about as solid as his argument. Renzi, whose problem was that he knew everything about everything, took the cigarette his colleague offered—not so much a gift as a bribe, like the match-stick that came along with it—but then countered the attack on two flanks. First, the situation in Europe didn't leave any room for anything else, and that should in his opinion take priority over all other news (It *is*, protested Yanofsky, interested more in blows struck in Buenos Aires boxing rings than Hitler's blitzkriegs, thus regarding the expansionism of the International Section with a similar horror to that of the rest of the world at the advance of the Nazis). Secondly, Renzi said that he wasn't the right man to cover the sport: although he knew a little about its history, he wasn't entirely familiar with what Yanofsky called the 'sporting' aspects on the board itself which, as he understood it, could get pretty complex. In an unacknowledged citation of his colleague Roberto Arlt, he reminded his interlocutor that Isaias Pleci used to hum to himself, went to the toilet forty times an hour, dropped cigarette ash onto the board and spilt his coffee. Everything was apparently fair game in the quest to win at chess. So it had to be considered a sport even in the unsporting sense of the term.

'Come on, you can't call a game where the players don't get up from their chairs a sport.'

'Getting up for the toilet is moving. Also, spending hours and hours sitting still requires stamina.'

'Fine. So it should go in the Entertainment Section, then. There's a reason they're holding it at the Politeama Theatre rather than Luna Park Stadium.'

Renzi hadn't spoken to the editor of the Entertainment Section but the argument had merit. However, he had orders to convince the Sports editor to cover the event, not to think, although this was requiring more effort of his little grey cells than he'd expected.

'You know that everything that goes into the Entertainment Section is paid for.'

'Yeah, in kind by the actresses.'

'They say the same thing about you and the boxers.'

'Very funny. So why don't they ask the Chess Federation for money?'

After explaining that the organization had gone into debt to pay for the tournament and didn't even have enough to send down the Americans, who'd won the previous one, Renzi returned to his earlier point, saying that if a pastime was disqualified as a sport because its players were sitting down, then horse racing shouldn't go into Yanofsky's section either—technically, jockeys just sat in their saddles.

'The jockey doesn't move,' Yanofsky conceded, even though their relative lack of movement was nothing compared to that of a chess player. 'But the horse does and they're joined together, like a boxer and his glove.'

'Or a chess player and his pieces. The knights, for instance.'

'But they move no further than an arm's length.'

The jockey didn't move, but they at least could fall and hurt themselves, Yanofsky added. A chess player, at the most, risked muscular atrophy from having to keep still for so long. And the point was that it couldn't be a sport if there was no risk of physical injury. Instead of poking holes in this newly improvised and just as dubious definition of competitive physical activity, Renzi fell once again into the trap of knowing too much. Like a ladies' man unable to keep his affairs to himself, not even from his wife, he said that the injuries caused by chess could be much more serious than those suffered in racing. Chess players might not be at risk of breaking a leg or an arm: it was their head they put on the line. The danger of splitting one's brain into 64 pieces was so high that some religions had even banned it, although that was at a time when it had been mixed with dice that randomly decided which pieces were to be moved and where. Still, there were always those who compared the game to alcohol and other drugs in a counter-argument to those who encouraged it as being good for the mind. In fact, they claimed that playing chess was just another form of imbecility, similar to an obsession with crosswords. Others saw chess as a far greater danger, believing it to be a metaphor for war, a generator of the violence that it purported to channel. After all, a classic story about the game, whose title Renzi would have liked to remember, featured a black man and a white man playing a game that had a violent ending: after the black man won the game, the white man killed him.

'Great, put it in the Crime Section then, they'll love it.'

'They'd only shove a bishop in my back,' said Renzi, who may have subconsciously remembered the name of the story: 'The Black Bishop'. 'I just offered them a great story about a suspected Nazi spy that they tried to foist back onto me because the guy's German. Imagine what they'd say if . . . '

Just then, the Crime editor happened to be passing by the sports desk accompanied by the general editor, Natalio Botana. Renzi stopped them. He wanted to talk to Botana, but first addressed the other man asking him whether he knew the name of the story where a white man kills a black man after a game of chess. The Crime editor told him to go ask someone from the Sunday supplement, much like someone sending an effeminate acquaintance to a club famous for harbouring homosexuals but then remembered that he'd recently read a mystery novel in which someone was killed with a white bishop. Before Renzi could ask, he added that he couldn't remember the name of the book or the author because he had no time for pansy crap and went off to his department.

'Talking about pansy crap,' Yanofsky said, 'footballers play a match, but chess is a game, like backgammon or cards. That's the difference between a sport and a non-sport.'

'My colleague Yanofsky and I are trying to define chess,' Renzi explained to Botana.

'Chess is a science,' Botana said to their surprise. 'Like maths. Or physics rather. Because physics has the random element, in quantum theory. Isn't that right? But in contrast to the sciences, it's completely useless.'

'Like art,' said Yanofsky.

'Or sport,' said Renzi.

'Sport is good for health.'

'Tell that to the balls of the guy who fought Godoy yesterday.'

Botana laughed at this duel of wits and they laughed along with him. And so the atmosphere grew more relaxed. But given they didn't have a Science Section, and certainly not a Philosophy one, one might say that they hadn't advanced a single square in their effort to resolve the issue. Renzi let it be known that he didn't think that debate was the best way to reach the newspaper's preferred solution, and that a compulsory mandate from on high was required. But he was unable to issue such an order to a colleague on the same hierarchical level. Botana thought for a couple of seconds before speaking.

'Let's do this,' he said eventually. 'You can play a quick, scientific game, five minutes each. The winner gets the tournament.'

'The winner?' Yanofsky exclaimed in a startled voice, even though it had been a long time since he'd played.

'The loser you mean,' said Renzi who was equally startled even though he knew more about the history of the game than the game itself. He hadn't played since he was a teenager. 'Neither of us wants it . . . '

But Botana was already leaving, saying as he went that the board, pieces and clock were in his office, and that they could ask his secretary to fetch them.

44

5

A DIRTY JOB

The first job that Heinz Magnus found in Argentina was, unsurprisingly, at a German company, the metalworking firm Segismuno Wolff S. A. He was charged with administrative work that he didn't enjoy and for which he was poorly paid. This comes out in the sworn statement he would present to the German authorities in his application for a pension in deutschmarks, a subsidy to compensate for the ravages of Nazism which included being forced to live in a country he clearly never fully adapted to; he continued to write in his mother tongue right up to the final line in his diary. According to this document, which I have right here in front of me, his salary was 170 Argentine pesos a month (which would rise to 175 the following month). This was the price of a 5-valve Victorette radio, 17.5 litre cans of Valiente oil from the El Luchador market or about 40 dollars at the official exchange rate. However one sliced it, it wasn't much money on which to support three people. So, almost certainly to pay debts that he'd incurred to finance his move overseas, Heinz seems to have tried to get more out of his former employer, an enterprise in which he was unsuccessful.

Today, something cracked inside me, he writes in his second diary entry, a year and a half after his arrival in Buenos Aires. *The faith by which the employee sees their employer as a genuine colleague. My dedication to G. R. was obviously greater than average . . .*

I'll interrupt this quote to move on to another from the previous year that shows that he really did put more into his work than he should have, or even wanted to:

We've had too much work for the past few days, weeks and months. The business is taking everything out of me. So much so that occasionally, but then for long periods of time, I lose all interest in setting a course for my life, or even considering it. Not even [Martin] Buber can get under my skin and I've let the very likely opportunity to begin a correspondence with him fall by the wayside. Not a good sign.

Getting back to 1937:

. . . after writing a long and detailed letter to Dr R, I received his reply today. It was friendly but with the clear subtext that I shouldn't write to him again. Of course, that's not what I was concerned about, but neither is it encouraging, especially when one considers the suffering I was forced to bear on behalf of that awful, imposing person. I should have written that many times, but this is the first time that I have.

We're very lucky to be living here, but the Almighty is making us pay a heavy price. Rarely have I yearned for

*economic independence as much as in the past few
months. Rarely have my thoughts been so taken up with
the notion of saving money. But there is the world as it is
and the world we wish to build.*

*If it were only down to me, I'd find a way to deal with
this awful person. If I were on my own I could bear it but
I'm suffering on behalf of three other people. My dear
mother, who works so hard and worries so much, who
has so much to do and is finding it so hard to adapt. My
father, who's 63, and finally Astarte, whose childhood is
being ruined; she suffers so much.*

Astarte was his sister Hertha. It's a strange nickname for two
reasons: Astarte was a goddess, the sister of Adonis (making it an
act of self-praise); and secondly because she was the goddess of
fertility and Hertha never had children (she'd been barren for several years following an abortion of an ectopic pregnancy). With
regard to the letter Heinz refers to, even though I'd much rather
it had been to Dr B. (do you know how much a signed letter from
Buber would be worth today, Grandpa?) it must have been
addressed to Dr Leo Robinsohn, founder, along with his brother
Max de Gebrüder Robinsohn, of a major clothing concern in
Hamburg for whom Magnus started work at the age of 17 after
graduating from the Talmud-Tora Realschule, the biggest Jewish
school in the north of Germany. He was a salesman for almost a
decade, specializing in textiles, a business in which his son (my
father) would later work. But what he wanted, and even
attempted, was to study at university:

Today I passed by brightly lit windows (he writes before
emigrating). *Windows that belong to a building I love. It*

represents the culmination of all my hopes and desires. And today, when I saw it in front of me, two worlds of sensations struggled for pre-eminence. I went there, to the university, so often to listen to people communicate with us. A veritable spirit settles over the lecture halls, hearts swell and breathe. During the pause, an interruption in the professor's lecture, we gave ourselves over to the realm of the spirit. But now the university is closed to Jews. Classrooms that once meant whole new worlds to us! Jews aren't welcome. But we go on . . . I truly wanted to study. Is my current job a vocation? Couldn't I serve humanity better in some other role? The university was once a refuge; I hope to find another in the course of my life.

My grandfather came across a similar refuge on the other side of the ocean, in La Plata, but once again entrance was denied.

It's a small, very pretty city (he says on 13th February 1939). *When I came to the university I felt the urge to study flow through my veins once more, as strong as ever.*

But he had to work, so he was only able to study when he got sick, twenty years later, by which time he'd turned somewhat agnostic and opted for Ancient Greek instead of Hebrew.

Back in Germany, his being Jewish had not only ruined his academic prospects, it also blocked his way to a promotion even before he was forced to flee.

My work situation grew more difficult every day (he says in his brief official autobiography written for the German authorities shortly before he died). *The decree stating that*

*an Aryan could not shake hands with Jews and should
refrain from talking or having direct contact with them
isolated me from my colleagues. It got to the point where
I was ignored, and, as I was the only Jewish salesman in
the textile warehouse it became almost impossible for me
to serve customers, so my income diminished.*

He then says that he refused to take part in the union meeting
of the *Arbeitsfront,* or Worker's Front, because it was held under
an anti-Semitic photograph of a dwarf (the Germans brandished
on their sleeve the kinds of things most of us would choose to
conceal) leading to 'incredible humiliation and harassment' and
the constant fear of being deported to a concentration camp (the
non-sporting version). The persecution continued at school: on a
trip to a weaving factory, he was attacked by 10 fellow high-
school students 'for no reason, or rather, for being Jewish'. It was
following that visit that my grandfather first wrote something
down in a notebook, the precursor to the diary, describing an
incident that appeared to disturb him even more.

*We went to the Bischoff & Rodatz factory. A man from
the company took us on a tour. He gave us some instructions and opened a door. We went into a large hall. Rows
of machines with people standing in front of them, loud
noise, a stink. 'Yes, we're paid by the piece,' a girl said in
answer to my question. The second hall was almost
exactly the same. I stopped in front of a working machine
and watched what the girls there do. Imagine having to
spend eight hours in front of a machine to make sure that
it's working properly; for no other reason, and if a thread*

comes off the roll, to put it back again. Eight hours non-stop. For years. Who's the machine here?

A school friend and I started to head back to the offices. He has a lame foot so can't walk very quickly. My feet are healthy and I can't walk at all, I don't have the heart to walk. I still see those girls; I see the living machines standing in front of the actual ones.

Getting back to the Robinsohn Brothers, the odd thing was that it was a Jewish company. One of the founders' sons, Hans Robinsohn, was an active member of the resistance. Later he had to go into exile in Denmark, where the firm had sent my grandfather for a few weeks to recover from the insomnia, migraines and heart problems that began when Hitler rose to power. The only reason he didn't stay there was his parents. He didn't seem able to leave them on their own. And maybe he didn't join Hans Robinsohn in the fight against the Nazis because he didn't have what's known as the fighting spirit, something that we'll try to rectify here (won't we, Grandpa?).

6
WORKING BACKWARD

Sonja Graf ordered another cognac and went on flicking through her copy of *Crítica*, which she'd bought because it had the most pictures. Occasionally she stopped at an article and tried to decipher it with the aid of a travel-sized Spanish–German dictionary. Small as it was, it contained all the words she looked up. She couldn't decide whether this indicated that it was a good dictionary or that her Spanish was terrible.

'Chained to his chair by rheumatism,' she read underneath a piece in which Savielly Tartakower predicted who would win the tournament ('Probably the Argentine team because they will surely have the best lodgings'). The photo that accompanied this medical report looked to be of one of the chess players who had travelled with her on the *Piriápolis*. There had been so many on the ship that she couldn't remember all their faces. She worked through the article word by word, trying to decipher who this unknown player was. Apparently he suffered from a condition that was anathema to his calling which required one to spend long periods sitting still. She knew the conjugations and endings of the different words and had enough grammar to be able to make up the rest with the dictionary and, as time passed, the exceptions too. Language wasn't so far removed from chess; it was just a question of degrees, a gap that shrunk further when one considered how each field worked. The irregular movement of the knight was the equivalent of irregular verbs: mastery of both was extremely useful.

She, too, found it difficult to stay chained to her chair, as the article so curiously put it. She preferred the effort of keeping an imaginary chessboard fixed in her mind, as though she were blind, to being forced to keep her body's centre of gravity stuck to a table and chair, sometimes all night. This impatience was the cause of her ferocious, kill-or-be-killed attacks and also her lack of attachment to her pieces, a reflection of her indifference to anything that supposedly belonged to her. Deep down, Sonja didn't believe in private property and certainly not ownership of other people as symbolized on the board by different pieces. The king was the only exception; she defended him instinctively, the way one defends their own life when in mortal danger. Was she secretly playing to lose, like the editors of the newspaper she held in her hands? That game, by the way, had finished as a draw and so the reports from the chess tournament appeared in the 'Miscellaneous' section. Not at all. Sonja couldn't conceive of playing chess for any reason other than winning, apart from anything else because it was too easy to allow yourself to be beaten, at least when you got to a certain level. When you played against a beginner, you played a dual role: you controlled both your pieces and those of your opponent, by suggestion.

'Take Dodd Pills for your kidneys and bladder today . . .' Sonja read at the end of the article and only then did she realize that the supposedly rheumatic passenger was in fact a surreptitious advertisement and to cap it off, for a product with which she was already familiar from home. She felt like an idiot, despite the fact that she'd been intelligent enough to detect a hoax in a language that had been completely foreign to her only a few weeks before.

She put down the evening edition to light a cigarette, had the waiter in the white coat with the shifty demeanour fill her glass back up like a doctor rationing out medicine—maybe this was another surreptitious advertisement—and tried to concentrate on the travel chess set on the table. It was a small wooden box in which each lid was one half of the board and the squares had little holes for inserting the pegs that extended from the bottom of the pieces. There was another line of holes on the side for the pieces that had been taken. She preferred the old-fashioned version to the modern ones with magnets, not because they were more stable (all real chess players can easily reassemble the board if it falls off the table, whatever position the pieces are in) but because it was harder to pick up and replace the pieces. This apparent disadvantage increased the pieces' gravity in both a figurative and literal sense, lending them a weight that Graf, in her suicidal indifference, no longer felt on other boards. Used as she was to carved wooden pieces that weighed little more than the fingers moving them from one side of the board to the other, playing with these tiny rooted trees was like moving menhirs around (this only sounds anachronistic unless one forgets that Obelix lived in classical times, even if the character was invented at the end of the 1950s). These deliberate shackles forced her to take more time over her moves, albeit subconsciously, before making her decision. Also, because taking a piece meant having to make double the effort of removing both and adding the taken one to the parade of holes at the side, which were much tighter because they got less use, every attack became a minor chore that tempered her suicidal impulses.

Another advantage of her travel chess set was that the pieces always stayed in the exact centre of the square. Sonja had a theory that even minor variations of position in each square revealed one's defensive or offensive intentions. This was especially true for the knight and the bishop, both capable of looking in a specific direction, thus indicating (or bluffing) the likely course of their next move. A piece's proximity to the edge of the neighbouring squares set off all manner of speculation and evermore complex strategies in response. But the more she dwelled on these hunches, the less effective they became. Her tea-leaf style of predictions tended to miss the mark and trusting them often distracted her from the simple complexity of how the pieces themselves were arranged. Her hypothesis about the revelatory nature of a piece's position brought more failure than success. She even used her eccentric technique actively, changing the position of her own pieces in order to throw off her opponent. But this didn't work either, *or not yet*, her more esoteric side whispered. The rest of her was sensible enough to realize that her ample experience in the world of chess told her that such superstitions were ridiculous.

As she desultorily moved the pieces around, she thought once again about how unfair it was that following the Anschluss, the Germans had added a couple of Austrian grand masters, Albert Becker and Erich Eliskases, to their team. How could they possibly have been invited after being so politely excluded from similar tournaments since 1933? She'd been avoiding these colleagues ever since she arrived, not because she had anything against them but because she didn't want to be reminded that there was nothing out of the ordinary about them, they were simply representing the wrong country. She would have hated having to make this hypocritical adjustment. Ultimately it would lead to alienating a nation from its inhabitants, as though it really did only consist of the flag and anthem, rivers and mountains. If nobody cared that the swastika had replaced the Eagle, in the end the entire fault of the war would be blamed on Adolf Hitler alone.

Adolf Hitler! Sonja Graf was still amazed at how the world continued to take the speeches and actions of a fanatic who openly railed against world peace, seriously. It had been so quick to treat him as an unimpeachable leader just when he was spouting the most barefaced of lies. While his speeches and policies against the Jews and in favour of German expansionism were ignored or dismissed, his false promises and cynical guarantees were taken as acts of good faith. There was no better evidence of this than his chess team, which included players from another country but excluded Jews from their own, forcing them to play for Palestine. Nothing could be a greater affront to the idea of the nation, which ought to be the defining characteristic of an Olympiad, and yet the Argentine organizers had overlooked this flagrant irregularity, regarding their magnanimous flexibility as a contribution to greater understanding between peoples.

Fools, Graf thought, and continued to practice endings on her travel board, as though she too were preparing for the imminent battle. Hitler had been getting his pieces into position for some time but only now was the world beginning to consider the urgency of taking a seat on the other side of the board. It was too late. To calculate the magnitude of the delay, she envisaged a game in which white was six moves ahead, one for every year that had passed since the awful events of 1933. Did black have a chance?

Placing herself on their side, she moved the Nazi pieces forward with an extended Ruy López opening, to which she responded with a dour Berlin defence: the German dictator would have a taste of his own medicine. But she immediately saw that black couldn't even hope for a draw, not unless the Nazis made a series of massive mistakes. This board-based evidence only spelled foreboding for whoever would take responsibility for defending democracy in this dark reality, even with the help of allies. The only way to win at such an initial disadvantage was to break the rules with some new, atomic weapon, the kind that hadn't been seen in chess for years.

It was because of these external (and internal) events that Sonja was convinced that the tournament couldn't possibly end well. They couldn't play without considering what was going on in Europe, even if the venue had been moved thousands of miles in an effort to distract the participants. It had apparently been organized to give a lesson to the troubled continent, showing how another great war could be fought between many different countries but in a civilized way, with no need for killing. One of the founding myths of chess, after all, was that it had been created to bloodlessly settle a territorial dispute between two ancient kings, and the current circumstances almost required that this initial purpose be revived; to make the metaphor a reality, so to speak.

'Fools!' Graf thought again, so vehemently that it almost came out as an exclamation, or perhaps she did say it under her breath. However, the idea that the game represented war made her more prudent about her exercises on the board, as though the fate of Europe, and the world, really did depend on it.

She tried to take the comparison seriously, to be as foolish as the organizers apparently were and some of the players had certainly revealed themselves to be when she'd brought it up. Adding inverted commas to soldiers massing at borders so that the pieces on the board lost their figurative meaning brought the game to life, as they say. Now it really was a matter of life and death. Every loss, leaving aside the ultimate one at the end of the game, shed blood and guts over the board, decimating, or simply wiping families out. Keeping in mind that the pawns, which couldn't take a backward step, would be prevented from having a second life after being killed by the enemy, gave them the status of kings, while the king himself became indistinguishable from the fingers moving him. But this kind of exaggerated identification didn't make the game any more exciting for Graf. Taking the metaphor to its logical extreme only made the pieces' movements meaningless, as often happens with forced, melodramatic comparisons. What should have seemed deeply tragic ended up being ridiculously absurd, perhaps because losing, although it might feel just as painful, even physically, didn't have the same irreversible consequences as it did on the battlefield. Or perhaps because winning meant being the last one standing on the field of the dead, after you've lost almost everything. In the famous words of the Duke of Wellington after the battle of Waterloo: 'With the exception of losing a battle, nothing is sadder than winning one.'

The trick wasn't working. Sonja was forced to forget her warrior mindset and focus on the actual fiction of the board. The pieces ceased to be a more-or-less appropriate metaphor for the world and instead became what they were, a world unto themselves, albeit an illusory one. Sonja's attention then found itself swallowed up by a force stronger than even the most painful reality: sleep. The only thing in the waking world that can produce its own narrative.

'Yes, queen. You lose.'

Graf looked up as though emerging from an inner struggle (her longing to play against men from her own country) and saw a young man draped in a coat that was too warm even for this winter's day. Under it was a yellow shirt too thin even for this overheated cafe, both of which were nonetheless excellent quality. The dishevelled but well-dressed youth's fists were clenched while his eyes were brimming over with chess.

'So you think I should move the rook instead?' Sonja asked without taking the cigarette from her lips.

'The king first.'

The young man's English was wholly chess-related, with just enough supplementary words to link the movements together. Graf wondered how many words he'd need, how many combinations of letters, numbers and colours, and then considered the possibility of inventing a language based around chess or at least a universal educational method for existing languages that ensured that one could express themselves to a sufficient degree wherever they went.

'How does white respond?'

'He moves his pawns, like that, but then you take them with your knight, and then the rook,' Czentovic finished, explaining how to escape a trap he himself had employed on the boat to Argentina.[2]

---

2 The shipboard game in *A Game of Chess* repeats that of Alexander Aleksándrovich Alekhine against the Russo-German player Efim Dimitrievich

While Sonja looked at him, trying to determine who this was standing in front of her, Czentovich spoke without taking his eyes off the board, as though he were talking to it, or using it as an intercom. He'd been observing the travel set from his table, where he'd sat down for a hot chocolate early that afternoon. Now he was convinced that she had to be taking part in the tournament of nations. He'd been wandering around the Politeama for days hoping to meet players, not that he knew what he was planning to do when he did. All he knew was that it was played in teams, a fact no one had told him beforehand (and it hadn't occurred to him to ask) and now he was desperately looking for a way into the competition.

'Would you like to sit down?' Sonja asked.

'White takes the pawn you didn't queen with the rook and then offers a draw.'

Stefan Zweig, or rather his narrator, says in the novel that Mirko Czentovic was strikingly arrogant. However, Graf saw immediately that his most dominant personality trait was shyness. The important thing was not to let oneself be fooled by the confidence with which he spoke about future moves; as though they belonged to a past only he had seen, and the associated implication that he would brook no contradiction. This exaggerated overconfidence wasn't arrogance but a classic sign of awkwardness in someone who only has experience in one area and thus invests all the vehemence they lack elsewhere into it. These

---

Bogoljubow at the tournament of Bad Pistyan in 1922. The decisive moment in that famous match came when Bogoljubow, playing black (the oil magnate McConner in the novel) was ready to queen a pawn but on the advice of a third party abstained, thus avoiding the trap set by Alekhine (Czentovic).

brusque assertions would then lapse into an embarrassed silence often misinterpreted as conceitedness.

Sonja briefly introduced herself and repeated her offer of a chair to which the boy finally responded by sitting down without a word. The German woman expanded a little upon her life story, but only when she got to the present and said what had brought her to Buenos Aires did her companion volunteer his name and profession, looking her in the eyes for the first time. Sonja was surprised to meet someone who described themselves as a chess player but didn't recognize her. There weren't that many people in the world who could make a living out of the pastime. She thought that the boy must be trying to impress her, another symptom of shyness that only reinforced the empathy she felt for this small, neatly drawn character. Was he trying to get a ticket to see the tournament, like the waiter had before? Whatever he was after, he seemed to know plenty about chess and his sudden appearance was somewhat miraculous. If she really wanted to put on a good performance in the tournament, Graf needed quality practice with someone who wasn't a prospective opponent. To find out whether this potential sparring partner (Yanofsky would not have approved of the metaphor) really was heaven-sent, she challenged him to a game on the travel board: the one they'd already begun, but in reverse.

'In reverse?'

'The first person to get to starting position wins.'

7
A MAGICAL CONVERSATION

In addition to his economic troubles, the other thing bothering my grandfather was his civil status. His divine sister Astarte, who was a year younger than him, was married already while he was still single. However, there did appear to be a prospect:

19th April 1938

Lili wants to come over.

24th April 1938

Today, I wrote to Lili in great detail and very firmly. I want her to come because I think we're a good fit.

The only other potential candidate for grandmother that my grandfather mentions in his diary; before he meets my grand-mother in a few months obviously (so long as we don't allow the facts to be undermined by the budding fictional fling with Miss Sonja Graf) was someone he apparently considered marrying when he was still in Germany:

31st January 1937

I can't stop puzzling over whether it would be right to marry Miss Fürst. At the moment she still lives in Vienna but there is some hope that she will come here [Hamburg]. *The big question is whether she is capable of loving someone, especially because I assume that she has already had intimate contact with two men. This is something that holds me back and also makes me wonder whether she will be faithful. Soon I shall be emigrating to Argentina, and, given that the women there are extraordinarily stupid, the question arises whether it might not be better to marry now. But can she, and will she, be willing to follow the path I want to and must follow—the religious one?*

A few pages earlier, Magnus explains how he came to meet this woman:

6th December 1936

The train continues to speed along. Further and further away from her. It's strange: the train runs every day and yet today is special. On it sits a person with whom I would like to talk again, with whom I'd like to be again and with whom there seems a good chance that I would get along. And perhaps more. The woman is pretty and has something feminine, maternal, about her. At the same time she also comes from a completely different social class to the one with which I am familiar, and my hopes of putting my ideas into practice with her mean that I suffer a little from her loss. If loss is the appropriate word. Of course I saw her on several occasions at the shop and spoke to her often but we only saw each other in private once. And just before she left. Now the train puffs along and she goes with it. The train speeds away, taking her away with it.

It's strange; if one wanted to, the train could not be stopped, it too has an untouchable power. All we can do is stay sitting without doing anything, wondering whether the hopes we harbour about a woman really would have been realized. Maybe they would have come to fruition, maybe not. One might have known, if they had had a closer relationship with her. We'll see what the letters have to say.

I don't know if that train passenger, who must be Miss Fürst, is also the Lili who toyed with the idea of coming to Argentina. I'd like to go back to the early hours of Monday, 28th August 1939, and ask my grandfather, as he slicked back his new haircut before heading to the Politeama in search of Sonja:

'Let's talk about *minas*, Grandpa.'

'I'm twenty-six, I don't even have children.'

'Well then, all the more reason to talk about *minas*.'

'*Minas* is *lunfardo* for girl and *lunfardo* is not regarded as polite speech. Even Roberto Arlt puts it in between inverted commas so as not to dirty himself.'

'Well then, let's talk about women, Heinz.'

'First we need to talk about your grasp of German, my dear grandson. Where do you come off telling people that I said that Argentine women were stupid (*dumm*)? I'd never met one! I meant that there weren't many of them (*dünn gesät*).'

'Oh, that was stupid of me.'

'If you say so.'

'The problem's your shitty handwriting, Grandpa. It's not me saying that, it's your son: he studied graphology.'

'Is that all he has to say about his father's private diary?'

'Apparently. He never bothered to read it.'

'He inherited my organizational skills but not my intellectual curiosity. It must have skipped a generation.'

'Talking about your intellectual curiosity: did you apply it to Miss Fürst?'

'A gentleman doesn't remember these things.'

'She's obviously the one from the train, isn't she?'

' . . . '

'Or is she Lili Lebach, the bookseller who published the first edition of *Schachnovelle*?!'

'Pigmalión was a good bookshop. A good name too.'

'No, it has to be the other one: she lived far away, she was from another world . . . '

'Good city, Vienna.'

'Marrying a Viennese woman would have established a connection with Stefan Zweig. I can't understand how you could have known that she'd been with other guys. Did she tell you, or did you find out from someone else?'

'All I can say is that she had intimate contact, the rest you have to work out yourself.'

'Is that why you wondered whether it was possible to love more than one person? I thought you were talking about yourself but obviously it was her.'

'I don't know what you're talking about.'

'So, not even you've read your own diary. Let me quote your entry from the 1st of January 1937:

So often the question has come up of how it is possible for someone to have loved someone, really loved them with everything they have, to then be able to love again, or maybe several times. To love someone else after they have separated from the first person. Of course, it's obvious these people respect love very much and regard it with the utmost sincerity and so 'love' relatively few people. But the idea that love is not unique is something I've often thought about.

'Were you trying to decide whether or not to marry a divorced woman?'

'They're just general questions, the kind you ask in a private diary. Haven't you ever wondered about things like that?'

'I don't know, I've never kept a private diary.'

'Why not?'

'Maybe because I've never been interested in that kind of writing.'

'What's the difference between that and a novel?'

'There's every difference. But it can be summed it thus: You can write a novel in diary format, but a diary can never be a novel. There's a chasm between the two.'

'I don't know. I always took my diaries very seriously. I regard them as my life's work.'

'I'm sure you do. I wasn't speaking pejoratively.'

'Come on, grandson, you're my direct relation.'

'I thought you didn't have children?'

'You started this absurd conversation, don't back out now.'

'You're right. We should bring it to an end before it gets out of hand. But first I'd like to know why you said that women were scarce in Argentina.'

'I meant German Jewish women. In the diaspora newspapers at the time, which I'll leave you along with my other papers, you'll see that all the personal ads written by single women state explicitly that they are willing to emigrate. They married so they could go into exile. Take a look:

Jewish woman, 40, good appearance, good family, very domestic, wishes to meet an upstanding Jewish gentleman, second wedding, followed by emigration.

Pleasant Jewish widow, 50, alone, 10,000.- seeks serious husband, a Jew by birth who must live overseas or have good connections overseas.

Young, educated, Jewish girl from Berlin, state degree, high intellectual level, from a comfortable home, seeks Jewish husband 28–35, in Paris if possible.

Pretty, independent Jewish lady. Blonde, 41, willing to be adaptable, a little property and schooled in domestic chores, seeks educated, cultured, single Jewish gentleman of means. Also emigration.

'I see. What about marrying someone who wasn't Jewish?'

'That was forbidden. Also it wasn't an option for me. Don't forget that I wanted to be a rabbi. Why do you ask?'

8

AN UNPRECEDENTED ENCOUNTER

Yanofsky couldn't understand why the Tournament of Nations was being held in a theatre or why people would go to watch the matches live but when he arrived that night and saw the number of people there, not to mention the fact that they paid up to 2 pesos for the right of admission (more than the cost of a large jar of Dodds pills 'to feel healthy and in control'. He'd written the copy himself), he felt like staying outside and covering the event as though it were international news.

'Tell me, sir, what's the attraction of watching two people sitting next to a board and moving wooden pieces around?'

'None that I can see. I'm only here because I'm going to commit a crime and I need an alibi.'

'And you, madam? Do you really have nothing better to do?'

'No, well, I got the wrong day. I thought they were showing something set in Algeria with that lovely girl, what's her name [Eva Duarte] but now that I'm here, I might as well stay.'

These were the only explanations for the long queue of men with slicked-back hair and made-up women, the former appreciably outnumbering the latter, thus providing another argument in favour of it being more of a sport than a show, he could conceive of. Of course, for a boxing match at Luna Park stadium there'd be fewer women still but that was because women hadn't yet started fighting themselves, unlike in chess. They made a vain attempt when men's boxing was made an Olympic sport. A photo had been hung up at the newspaper offices showing two American women boxers during an exhibition bout at the turn of the century, both swaddled in a kind of full-body petticoat that covered their arms and went halfway up their neck. If only they'd fought half-naked like the men! But Yanofsky was against discrimination: if they wanted to hit each other, let them. And they could do it pretty well when they wanted to. In his trips to the brothel, he'd seen ladies face up to each other in full-fledged fist fights, none of your hair-pulling or scratching there. It was thanks to these brief exhibitions (a man always came to break them up, probably to preserve his status as the only one allowed to hand out beatings) that he knew that many of them could easily have got the best of him; and not just the flabby forty-year-old that years of smoking and a sedentary lifestyle had turned him into, but even the rosy-cheeked, wiry kid who would have enthusiastically got into boxing in his native Ukraine. If only he too hadn't been a victim of discrimination. Not because he was a woman, of course, but because he was Jewish. In his country, if one could call that gigantic plaything of neighbouring countries, even Poland, a rather popular plaything in its own right, that. This was why he had always been so apathetic about war games; he knew that he'd always be on the losing side. In his big *paisucho*, it seemed obvious that a Jew couldn't play that sport or any other (except for chess), so much so that until he got to Argentina he didn't believe that boxers of his race existed.

Only when he started to work for newspapers, first in the mail room and later as a reporter, first at *La Razón* and later at *Crítica* (first in the International Section and later in Sports Section), did he begin to discover that the world of boxing was full of Jews. Until fairly recently, the diaspora had outnumbered even the Italians and Irish, in America at least. The problem was working out who was who behind their pseudonyms. The first to surprise Yanofsky was Benjamin Leiner, or Benny Leonard, about whom he first wrote to cover his retirement. That catastrophic fight of October 1932 in which a slow, balding Benny ruined a proud and lengthy record of never having hit the canvas with a brutal knock-out would in contrast lead to Yanofsky's triumphant passage from the International to the Sports Section. He'd been assigned to cover the fight and in his desperation to fill up the space he'd been given—not a single cable had arrived about it—it occurred to him to dig around in the archive, where he discovered that Leonard was from a Jewish ghetto in Manhattan. He excitedly reported this news to the editor, who told him irritably that he was stating the obvious:

'What difference does it make?' he asked, somewhat rhetorically.

'None, I suppose,' Yanofsky stammered in confusion. But then he recovered his composure. 'Or rather it does. People like to know whether a boxer is black or Italian, don't they?'

'They're not horses.'

This was one of those editors ashamed of the section they've been assigned to run. He'd probably aspired to more, the International Section maybe, where Yanofsky had just come from and his inferiority complex led him to assume that everyone was always telling him how to do his job. Yanofsky would find out later (he was always late!) about another likely reason for the editor's irritability: he himself was a Jew hiding behind another name, and he'd even married a gentile. In any case, the editor's gruff reaction and the pleasure he'd taken in writing his first real sports piece (before that, he'd just summarized cables) inspired him to lobby for a transfer to another section, even if that meant a demotion, so as to rise again there as quickly as possible, even if that meant undermining a fellow Jew. Five years later, he'd successfully achieved both goals and he celebrated the moment with a profile of his favourite boxer, his fellow Ukrainian Dover-Ber David Rosofsky, aka Barney Ross.

By now he'd also managed to track down several local Jewish boxers such as David Werner and Jacobo Stern with a vague plan to one day write a book on the subject (but what was the subject exactly?). He'd also started to become a regular at Luna Park and other stadiums in the city and across the country, mostly in the dual role of reporter and aspiring manager looking to discover a rookie pugilist. Sometimes it was just for pleasure. Whenever he stepped inside one of the venues, he felt the same shiver as he had the first time his father had taken him to see a professional fight, only now in a lesser, almost absurdist version: a kind of visceral revulsion for the spectacle he had come to witness. Just as the attraction to combat, something morally inhuman, must date back to the beginning of humanity, the result was a sense of guilt similar perhaps to the shudder that a gambler feels when entering a casino. *How can this excite me*? he thought, like a good Christian just before indulging in a bout of adultery. The sight of two men beating each other's brains out under the eager, even lustful gaze of a horde of bloodthirsty lunatics? On that first occasion, the shock had lasted well into the second round until, little by little, he got caught up in the general excitement and ended up demanding the death of one of the fighters. And the feeling always came back, although it lasted for shorter and shorter amounts of time. Now it was a kind of reflex, the shiver of someone standing in a luke-warm shower.

Yanofksy felt something similar now upon entering the Politeama, and it confused him because he could see no similarities whatsoever. From the ornate building to the well-dressed audience, it all seemed the exact opposite to an evening of boxing. To avoid paying the entrance fee, he told them that he was a 'special correspondent', although he silently added 'boxing, football and other real sports' in between the 'special' and 'correspondent', promising that his articles would mention the complaint of the organizers about all the people who had snuck in without paying ('Tell all those Portuguese[3] that the Chess Federation still has a debt of 150,000 pesos, maybe that'll loosen their pockets.')

'The complete list of players by team with all the matches in the preliminary round along with spaces to mark the results?' a kid with bulging eyes but a sleepy expression was standing in his way in a violet uniform and round cap that made him look like a cinema usher.

'Don't you mean "games"?' Yanofsky asked worriedly.

The boy narrowed his eyes, making him look even more dreamy and lackadaisical. The journalist just reached out and thanked him.

'That'll be 10 cents, sir.' Now the boy didn't seem lackadaisical at all.

---

3 An unfortunate Lunfardo term for people who avoid an entrance fee. (Note at the request of the editor and to avoid the wrath of the Luso-Argentine Association.)

Yanofsky showed him the brown label he'd pinned to his jacket that identified him as a journalist, at which the boy enquired if he was specialized. Yanofsky decided that his professional dignity was worth at least 50 cents and flipped him a coin.

Skimming through the Homeric line-up of players ready to do battle (the horse-shaped logo for the tournament could easily be that of Troy!) he wondered whether close examination of the different publications covering the event wouldn't reveal variations in the trickier names (the scale went: tricky, very tricky and Slavic), probably on the same page. Obviously because of his own surname, Yanofsky was sensitive to such difficulties and took special care over spelling in his own section. He made sure that even the substitutes' names were printed correctly. Although he was there representing another section, he was going to stay true to the principle that there was nothing worse than misspelling someone's name. If he ever slipped, it was because of a lack of clear rules (how do you know how to spell a Bulgarian name if it's never been pronounced in another language?) but at least he committed to making the same mistake throughout the tournament.

'Abraham Janowski?' he read out in surprise.

'The Canadian Sensation,' a man with a scruffy white beard and hair told him. 'He's second board at just 15 years old.'

Yanofsky immediately saw that this was one of these jovial but rather overbearing old men who like to make friends at sporting events. The kind who one also often saw at boxing matches (another similarity). Although he generally tried to avoid these irritating enthusiasts, on this occasion he saw that the old man might be useful.

'Second board . . .'

'But the rest of the team isn't that strong,' his companion went on quietly, looking to either side in the hopes that someone else might be listening. 'I think this'll be between the Germans and the Poles. Quite the coincidence, don't you think?'

It took Yanofksy a few moments to realize that he was referring to events in Europe, partly because he wasn't paying much attention and partly because it didn't occur to him that chess could have any bearing on the outside world at all. And partly also because he was still thinking about Janowski.

'This Janowski . . .'

'Yanofski, with a *y* and an *f*, they misspelt it. He's playing against Sor Thomas Barry at one of the tables at the back, come on.'

The man (had he said 'Sor' instead of 'Sir'?) led him along the long horseshoe-shaped passage, on either side of which people squeezed in to see the players sitting at their tables, which were set out in three rows, a double one in the centre of the hall and two single ones along the seats at the side. The ropes strung out in rectangles to separate the audience from the players were another thing the two sporting events had in common, as were the national coats of arms and the oversized banners hanging all over the place, reminiscent of international fights at Luna Park.

When they got to the sector where the stage usually was and now where the passage made its turn, the crowd was so thick that you couldn't see the players, let alone the board, not even on tiptoes. Yanofsky opined that they should have raised the 'ringside' but his companion didn't understand the allusion, or at least didn't find it amusing. What he did do, with surprising light-footedness for his age, was lead him to the second-floor balcony from where

Yanofsky could view the table through binoculars, which his new friend also supplied.

'Do you think he looks like me?' Yanofsky asked, handing the binoculars back to their owner so he could provide an educated answer (he thought so, a little).

'Why do you ask?' he said, fiddling with the knobs (although he was actually looking through the instrument backward).

'Because we share a surname.'

'Oh. But perhaps it's one of those strange-sounding names that turn out to be like Smith or Fernandez in their home country, like mine?' suggested the old man, possessor of an unmistakeable first name.

It wasn't such a common name, but it wasn't unique enough to lead one immediately to assume they were related, Yanofsky was forced to admit. He decided to forget about family business and concentrate on his professional duty, which was to write something colourful about the event. Also, he needed to talk to Capablanca. The editor in chief had learnt that *El Mundo* had hired Alekhine and *La Razón* Tartakower to write exclusively about the tournament for them and didn't want his paper to be left out. The problem was that Yanofsky didn't know what Capablanca looked like and was embarrassed to ask.

'Isn't Capablanca playing today?'

'Doesn't look like it, does it?' answered his companion, going along with a joke Yanofsky hadn't made.

He'd only find out what the old man had meant the next day when Capablanca sent them his first article, in which he explained why he'd only been able to draw with an apparently lesser player, Moshe Czerniak from Palestine:

My friends and fans are undoubtedly thinking that I should have won and they're probably right . . . On the technical side I may have been a little weak, a flaw from which I've been suffering for some time. But it's easily understandable if you take into account that I have been distracted by other interests that have nothing to do with chess. Sometimes whole months go by at a time when I don't get a chance to sit down at a board . . . All I can say is that after a couple of months' proper training I'll be ready to face, and I believe beat, any rival [i.e. Alekhine, who owes me a rematch after '27]. And I'm ready and willing to do that for any winner takes all prize that might be on offer [i.e. Alekhine, if he thinks he's up to it].

As though the inevitable passage of time, which today allows us to cite Capablanca's articles in *Crítica*, worked retro-prospectively in Yanofksy's mind, he realized that each team had its own flag. All he had to do was find Cuba's to narrow down his search to four people. And given that Capablanca had to be first board, bingo (checkmate)!

'*Look at the beautiful lady . . .*' said old man Fernández, who looked worried that his companion was about to abandon him. '*I mean the beautiful lady of chess. A piece has only one fate and the art of the chess player is to make sure that that sole occurrence happens: with exquisite, subtle technique, the characters on the board must come to life.*'

The image of the pieces becoming human made Yanofsky think of a giant chess set in which the pieces were played by humans, although it wasn't clear who was moving the pieces (God!). Whoever it was, it would be a sight to see, or even to pay to see. He needed to share the idea with the owner of the newspaper to see if there was something that could be made out of it.

'You've given me a great idea,' he said gratefully to the old man with the binoculars, who would also be mentioned in his sketches.

'The idea already lay dormant inside you, I just woke it up,' he replied, freely giving up any claim he might have had to the rights. 'If we could read the players' minds, we'd find that the same often happens with them. They think and think but the move they eventually decide to make is inspired by something outside them, a distraction.'[4]

Before going back down to the ground floor in search of the Cuban table, Yanofsky stopped in the first-floor foyer, intrigued by the crowd of people that had gathered there. Some enormous chessboards, sponsored by the YPF oil company, had been hung in a small room, where the leading games were being followed and commented on. These included Capablanca's; telling him exactly which table to look for (next to the one being occupied by his namesake, which explained why there were so many people crowded around it). The procedure was like that of a headquarters in wartime: someone called out the moves relayed to them from the hall and a third person moved the cardboard pieces from one

---

4 Macedonio Fernández's statement is correct. The third board on the Dutch team, Adriaan De Groot, had made use of the trip on the *Piriápolis* to perform some famous experiments, the results of which would be published after the war under the title *Thought and Choices in Chess*. De Groot sat down to play with Lodewik Prins, the fourth board, and made him say out loud, the way a psychoanalyst has their patients describe their dreams, everything he was thinking before he made a move. In the log for one of these experiments, it shows that after considering all the different possibilities for half an hour, the dinner gong jolted him into a spontaneous move that had just occurred to him.

square to another. The commentator, in his sixties with the name and bearing of a former boxer, 'Benito Villegas', was glorying in vernacular chess-speak. He was described as a 'pony enthusiast'— not because he liked the track, but for his love of knights. Apparently he was willing to lose a game just to prove that knights were superior to bishops. In addition to the retired chess-player's official commentary (he speculated ahead of each move to such a degree that you'd have needed an alternative board just to keep up, not that losing track of the pieces was without its charm, like a stray punch deciding the fight out of nowhere), the rest of the crowd were sharing their own opinions. They seemed far more interested in gossiping than in the chess matches per se. During the time it took a player to make a move, the spectators of this live broadcast had already come up with a thousand better options. Again, this was not unlike the crowd between rounds at a boxing match. Although the quibbles and protests of the geniuses in the foyer were beyond him, Yanofsky nonetheless suspected that if the players listened to them they'd never win (he'd put that in his article, although, out of humility, he'd attribute it to someone else). Back at ground level, his notes continued to adopt a negative, mocking tone. He described chess as 'the scientific indulgence of silence' and the players as 'a riposte to the febrile activity of the times', giving the hall the air of 'a church during Easter week' (he probably meant Passover), while the audience followed the 'stations', shuffling from table to table. He gleefully noted the oversized matches that the Norwegian player Haakon Opsahl used to light his cigars and the urchin collecting players' autographs on a cardboard board. He also observed that 'the women's tournament is not a bastion of high fashion. Thick sweaters and garish outfits are the norm'. Writing about the 'little

German woman'—Graf, and unable to mention her legs, he described her '*garçon* haircut' and suggested that she played under no flag 'because she's not a pure Aryan', a point in her favour.

The tenor of these 'impressions', which he would publish under the pseudonym 'The White King' (in a veiled tribute to an albino boxer he'd met on one of his trips around the country who he'd considered representing him not so much for his boxing talent as the striking colour of his skin), may have been snide and jokey, an obligatory style at the newspaper where he worked, but the truth was that Yanofsky was enjoying himself. He even regretted a little having used an interview a few days ago with Paul Keres to include the affirmation that chess made it harder to find a girlfriend while real men played sport, being a given that chess didn't count in that category.

As the night went on, another significant coincidence by the way; he couldn't think of another sport that was preferably played at night other than boxing: as it got closer to midnight and the tension in the air increased along with the cloud of cigarette smoke, Yanofsky felt more and more at home. He even began to follow one of the games, later describing the players as 'pitting their skills against each other, as a boxing reporter might say'. He enjoyed the match between Ernst Sorensen and Lodewijk Prins (the guy from the experiment) and even the fact that it ended in a draw, a result rarely seen in boxing. He was surprised to find himself thinking that it wouldn't be a bad idea if it happened a little more.

He also surprised himself with the thought that an exchange of pieces was very similar to an exchange of blows: they got more exciting the longer they went on and one of the players always ended up in better shape than the other, much as the one at a disadvantage might try to conceal it. The image could also be applied to moves that took no pieces at all, which were like feints or missed jabs; failed attacks on serried defences. Generally, the development of these two fluctuating but identical teams of black and white seemed a slowed-down, underwater version of the sweaty bodies in two-colour shorts that locked horns in the ring. It was most obvious when there was no result, when neither had managed to really draw blood, although they'd done plenty of damage to the spectacle.

And there was more. Although there were no interruptions in chess, there were brief rounds between different pieces in certain areas of the board until the action moved on, just like in the ring. Outright assaults by necessity left the defence exposed while who-ever dominated the centre dominated the match; both these aspects reminded him of his favourite sport. Looking at it from the opposite perspective, he saw that some forms of punches in boxing were analogous to the wooden pieces, which is why they had their own names. At one point in the night, he imagined a boxing ring with squares (it was eight by eight, after all, if one included the ropes) and board with no visible marks (except for the ropes around it) and only because of his limited imagination (living chess pieces and undercover advertisements had both been done before) did it not occur to him to combine the two sports with three minutes in the ring followed by three minutes at the board, as would occur at the beginning of the following century with *Schachboxen* in Germany. He regretted not having come on the first night and promised himself that he'd be there for the rest (he wouldn't).

At around midnight, the Yanofsky vs Najdorf game came to an end and Yanofksy, our Yanofksy, the fictional, or almost fic-tional one, approached the real one. Only then did he realize that the boy was young enough to be his son as well as his brother. Because he couldn't think what to say, he just took a small photo of his father he kept in his wallet, which was such good quality that even after a quarter of a century the only thing that had aged was the haircut of the subject (the photo of my grandfather which I used to describe his haircut in the previous chapter is proof of this: just as sharp and shiny three-quarters of a century after it was taken). The younger Yanofsky, who'd just signed the urchin autograph hunter's cardboard board, took him for another autograph hunter and accepted it, surprised (but not that surprised) that someone already had a photograph of him. Only when a protective instinct (to preserve a memory) made the older man brusquely grab the photograph back did the young man look at it more closely.

'That's my father!' the Canadian exclaimed in English.

'Mine too!' said the Ukrainian in gibberish.

The conversation continued by means of gestures, the last of which must have been the hug with which their unexpected reunion was sealed according to the account that hovers over this little fiction. But in our experience we know that such novel-type climaxes are more likely to arise in the heat of the story; expressions of wish-fulfilment or an emotional need to tie up loose ends, than to actually happen. Paradoxically, they're proof that something was real, even if it may not have occurred.

For whatever reason, they split up pretty quickly. The lack of a common language concealed rather elegantly the fact that the boy had little interest in talking to his half-brother, as would later become apparent (or not) in his book of omissions *Chess between Punches*, as Yanofsky would have preferred the title to be.

'You share a surname, Yano,' a former colleague at *La Razón*, the aforementioned 'Public Spectator Number One', noted a second after saying hello.

'I've just discovered that he's my brother,' Yanofsky answered, stirred not so much by the encounter as by the clear evidence that his father had got on with his life without ever getting in touch with his elder son.

'You're kidding me!'

'Half-brother, actually.'

'You're half-kidding me!'

After being surprised at how long he had had to wait to say hello to a former colleague as he chattered on for no good reason with an unknown player, the writer from *La Razón* was now stunned that the reunion had been so short. And especially at the reaction of the boy, which didn't seem appropriate at all. He'd shown no more emotion at the discovery of a long-lost relative in a remote country than he would have at seeing a neighbour's pet outside his house. Maybe it was his age, which has little time for nostalgia, or the fact he was a chess player, who weren't exactly known for being demonstrative. Whatever the reason, the momentous event didn't seem to have registered, and in the knowledge that his colleague wouldn't be able to mention it because he wasn't famous enough to talk about himself in the newspaper, he promised himself that he'd dedicate a few lines to it in his. That way, it wouldn't be lost like a good move one eventually decides against making.

9

BETWEEN ROBOTS AND HUMANS

My grandfather would have liked to feature in the previous chapter but he'd fallen asleep. He hadn't quite got used to the Argentine, or rather Spanish, habit of extending one's day well into the following one and then cutting it in half for several hours. He didn't take siestas and at night he collapsed in exhaustion after an early dinner, which was always kosher.

> *Kosher food sometimes has its amusing side* (he writes in his first entry written in Buenos Aires in late 1937). *After eating milk products, there was a pudding that was also made with milk. Given we generally eat meat, mother didn't think of that and I didn't get mine. When I asked why, I was told that it was made with milk but as I hadn't had meat before I said that there was no problem.*

And today was no different: he fell asleep before ten o'clock as usual and when he got up to pee after midnight—I'd like to say because he'd drunk so much mate, Salus mate being the official mate of the chess championship, or pretender to the title at least, to judge from an advertisement that appeared to coincide with the tournament:

SALUS, as graciously hospitable hosts, will be supplying mate to the best chess players in the world. Every delegate at the premiere chess tournament on earth has been given a mate gourd, a bombilla and a can of SALUS mate tea.

Some will take them back to their home country as a gift, a memento of a healthy Argentine pastime, but many others will be initiated into the Argentinian habit of drinking mate and discover the greater lucidity and activity that SALUS stimulates in the mind.

SALUS satisfies, keeps alcohol at bay, makes the home more welcoming, makes life more affordable and protecs [sic] one's salus [not sic].

For the Homeland!

YERBA SALUS

Mackinnon & Coelho LTDA. S. A [Yeah!]

... before the ad break, I was saying that though I'd like to say in fellowship with my British and Portuguese brethren that my grandfather got up in the night because he'd overdone the Salus mate, the truth is that he probably never tried it in his life. Not that brand or any other.

And yet, he decided not to go back to bed. Instead, he got dressed and went out. Again, I'd like to say that this was at least partly because he liked chess but that would be being economical with the truth: I have no evidence that he even knew how to play. His path was guided solely by the urge to see the German woman with the boy's haircut again, the hope of an intimate encounter with her (what that means, exactly, is yet to be seen) and finally the audacious intention of suggesting that she stay in Argentina once the tournament was over (something that she would in fact do, as both we and history have seen). The fact she wasn't Jewish was an issue, a big issue, but it could be resolved through a *guiur*, or conversion. And although that wasn't ideal, what was now in poor Heinz's life?

The streets were dark and lonely, but too cold for Heinz to be worried about getting mugged. The damp air was freezing, making him feel as though he was back in his home city of Hamburg where he often walked at night, in that case not because it was late but because the sun went down much earlier. After a long walk, he got to a recently expanded part of Calle Corrientes and was dazzled by the lights in both the literal and figurative sense. He still found it scandalous that they went to the expense of keeping the streets lit all night. Of course, in this country people did walk around until dawn but the odd streetlamp would have been enough to help them find their way. He could already see the neon knight in the distance, the symbol of the International Chess Federation and thus of the tournament (another had been set up in the Plaza de Mayo. People often mistook it for an advertisement for a country fair.)

He got to the building with the Art Deco (beneath it lay nineteenth-century bricks) facade at a quarter to two in the morning and found that it was closed. Like every family man who regarded 'nightlife' as a homogenous entity, he was surprised that something that had begun at night didn't come to an end when the sun came up but, rather, at some vague intermediary hour. The disappointment did have its reassuring side, however, because it made him feel like a veritable night owl, something he'd only experienced in an unpleasant sense: during bouts of insomnia, which were frequent in spite of the Placidón pills (a sedative that, if you'll indulge us with another brief commercial break, he'd chosen because of its erudite advertisement):

Achilles, the hero of the Iliad, was feared for his irritability, which led him often to take cruel revenge. Today, it's essential that we keep our temper in check.

He was about to go back, almost pleased that he had been thwarted by fate, a rival so imposing that it didn't even hurt to lose to him; he was about to go home, if one could describe the set of unwelcoming rooms he occupied along with his parents as such, in a city still in its infancy when he moved to it; he was really about to leave, not even held back by the excuse of lighting a cigarette before setting out (then what was holding him back?) when Benito Villegas came out of the theatre and, seeing that my grandfather was lost (like most chess players when they got more than a few feet away from the board), told him that everyone had gone, as usual, to the Chantecler, waving vaguely in the opposite direction to the one he subsequently set off in.

Magnus walked a few desultory steps towards the corner, sure that he'd never find the place; he couldn't even remember the name well enough to ask properly (if 'name' was the right term for a bastardization of *chante claire*). It was only because the lights of the nightclub on Calle Paraná could be seen from the corner that Heinz didn't go back to the place he shouldn't ever have left if he had any feeling for the family he was supposed to be starting after he met my grandmother.

As soon as he stepped through the door, the smoke and tango leapt up at his neck like a dog gleefully welcoming home its master. That is, if Heinz liked dogs, which seems unlikely given he never had one. So: like a dog attacking an intruder. My grandfather can't have liked tango either, or at least I didn't inherit any tango records. As I said before, he didn't smoke and I don't believe he drank (although there is a curious entry during his summer holidays that year that reads: 'Today I slept for a long time, took photos and read with bread and wine'). After a quick scan of the packed club, a smaller version of the Politeama with balconies and a stage, he was unable to find the chess player he was looking for, so he had every reason to leave the same way he'd come in.

But it was warm, Grandpa, and that always makes it tempting to stay a little while longer, doesn't it? Also, Magnus felt more awake than ever, as though he'd snorted a line of the cocaine that was probably doing the rounds of the tables and bathrooms. He headed straight for the latter, or thought he did; he'd taken off his fogged-up glasses, and, when he put them back on, he realized that he was in fact standing at the door to the kitchen. Then he realized that he didn't need to use the facilities after all. He sat down in the first free chair he found, at a table that was occupied for the same reason he'd stayed, to judge by the occupant's lack of a coat. Or maybe he'd left it on a peg at the entrance, a convenience that Heinz hadn't even trusted in Hamburg, not that he'd ever heard of anyone actually stealing anything. The waiter came over right away, more mistrustful than solicitous, perhaps because his customer was looking surly; i.e. not drunk, or perhaps because his companion was only drinking a cup of coffee (with its little glass of water, which people serve here without your having to ask for it, a detail that my grandfather found very charming). To the sceptic in the white coat and bow tie who had come over in a falsely servile manner, my grandfather pointed to the cup in front of his new partner-in-crime like someone referring to an article of jurisprudence that absolves them of all guilt, or even the possibility of being charged.

'I played with you thrice and came out on top—two–one,' he heard from the neighbouring table (but we would read in the book *Najdorf by Najdorf*, written by the chess player's daughter).

'That's not true,' he heard in reply, which was in German (the language Alekhine claimed to think in when playing chess). 'We've played twice and both were draws. And in one of those games you got lucky.'

Seeing that his companion was staring at the man as though he were a god (actually, he thought 'as though he were in love'), Heinz turned to look at them too. Neither of them seemed to mind; they were almost asking for an audience, or expecting one. They tended to be the centre of attention in crowds.

'No, sir. We've played three times,' insisted the first speaker, Moisés Mendel Najdorf, about whom the following anecdote would later be told:

At noon one day in the Polish embassy, Najdorf would tell the ambassador, the consul and I—Juan Carlos Gómez, a friend of Witold Gombrowicz—a story with a moral at the end. It seems that Najdorf, a member of the Polish chess team that came to Argentina to compete in the '39 Olympiad, was responsible for the death of another Jewish chess player. Or so he said.

Najdorf's place in the team was assured before the final match of the selection tournament held in Poland but his opponent could only get in the team if he beat Najdorf. So the opponent's wife asked Najdorf's wife to ask him to let him win. Najdorf refused, his Jewish colleague stayed in Poland and the Germans killed him in a concentration camp.

When Najdorf came to the end of the story, which had had the desired dramatic effect, the consul spoke up; an ominous expression had come over his face. His eyes gleamed with cunning intelligence. He told Najdorf not to worry, he wasn't responsible for the tragedy, fate was. If Najdorf had let the man win, his Jewish counterpart would have been saved but the man who did come to Argentina with him, who was also Jewish, would have died instead. We drank some vodka and moved on to the next tale.

'In 1929 [ten years earlier] you arranged an exhibition of thirty simultaneous matches plus two blind ones, and I played in one of the latter,' Najdorf said.

'Thirty matches plus two more blind ones . . .' the other man said, thinking, his glass of whisky frozen at his lips. 'Did you sacrifice your rook at g7? That was you? You're right!'

They toasted each other and then their audience, who laughed and applauded the exchange. Just then the orchestra started a new piece and the waiter came over with two cups of coffee. Magnus raised his hand to protest that he'd brought one too many, but on seeing his companion's grateful smile when the waiter passed him his refill he adapted the gesture into a cordial invitation.

'The man, Alekhine, great champion, world champion,' Mirko Czentovich informed his benefactor by way of thanks.

In addition to this information, which he took a while to process (champion of what? Ah, right), Heinz was pleased to hear the poor quality of the man's English, which made him feel like a British gentleman in comparison. In May the previous year, he'd started taking classes at the British Cultural Centre and a month later he was writing entries in the language of Shakespeare, or at least the *Buenos Aires Herald*. See, for instance, the following entry for the 26th of June, describing a wonderful moment for a lover of books:

> *This night one of my wishes was fulfilled; I bought the* Oxford Dictionary. *Nearly for one week I visited all booksellers in order to learn the price of this book or to succeed in getting a second-hand one. But whilst the mayority of the 10 or 15 booksellers where I was asking for didn't possess it at all, neither new nor used, 2 or 3 of them offered it at a price of \$(?)7. So I was glad after my journey through Buenos Aires to obtain still the dictionary at this price, and now begins a new epoch in my study of the English language.*

His first year had been a great success and not just because he got good marks. Having been prevented from going to university, after years, or rather a lifetime of doing nothing but work, Heinz was finally able to dedicate himself to what he loved the most: study.

2nd April 1936

Yesterday I said farewell. I said farewell to my ideals, to my hopes, to my books. I have been depressed for days. Oppressed by all the hopes that now lie beneath rubble. I was desperate for the truth, for a revelation ... but not all the philosophy or religion in the world can offer a more accurate vision of humanity. Man's existence only appears to make sense when seen in relation to men or things. But woe is me if I ever come to believe that this is the meaning of all existence! Of course it's brazen to wonder about the meaning of life, but without an answer I cannot truly live or achieve genuine awareness. Everything one does, everything one creates, lacks meaning if the meaning of everything remains hidden. I don't feel anchored to this world, to this life. I feel no joy or will to live or fear of death; I can't live simply because I'm here or take something just because it's given to me. I want to achieve something. But the years that were supposed to guide me towards that goal are now behind me and a dark night casts its shadow over me. And thus I became aware a step away from awareness: existing within the sphere where one cannot and does not want to seek the meaning of life. I have parents and my sense of duty demands that I take care of them. And I can't achieve that without a relatively optimistic outlook.

Yesterday I emptied out my work locker. The Torah, Buber's translation, philosophy books, the history of the evolution of the world . . . Everything was put into storage and its place was taken up by the English language and commercial texts along with books in Spanish. My world is sinking and another world, a more unpleasant one, has taken hold of me and made me its own. And I must establish a relationship with it, I must adapt to this new world.

Once again, I have braced myself to strive towards the objective of 'making a career' for myself, once again I have put all my energy into keeping myself alive because, yes, because the meaning of life can never be to negate oneself or the world. There is no doubt that that is not the meaning but if one can go on, if they can stand the pain of not knowing, only time will tell.

'I continue to be amazed by your sense of filial duty,' I say, sitting down at the table in the Chantecler and taking advantage of the fact that Czentovich isn't the most talkative person in the world. 'It reminds me of my maternal grandmother who, by the way, lived in Hamburg at the time, perhaps you have met her?'

'You'd love that, wouldn't you? That way you could invent a love story for your little novel.'

'Actually, I was thinking that Grandma might have been the girl from the train. I don't know if there was anything pretty or maternal about her but I know that she lived in the countryside, so was from a 'completely different' social class to yours. What did those letters you were waiting on say in the end?'

'*None of your business.*'

'Fine, I see that your English classes are going well at least. Tell me, did you ever go to the Jewish hospital in Hamburg?'

'The one where your maternal grandmother worked? I'm sorry to say that I wouldn't have met her even if I had been admitted, the dates don't work out. I left Hamburg in 1937 and she got there in 1938.'

'Did you know that she also kept a diary? Just for a few days, also written on the ship that brought her over from Europe. It was only four or five pages but it talks about Auschwitz and things.'

'You mean that it's much more interesting than the hundreds of pages I wrote because I was never sent to a concentration camp?'

'You can't compare the two. Your entry for the 25th of May 1938, which is full of words in Spanish, seems more eloquent to me than all the books about Nazis in Argentina.'

'. . . ?'

I was in the Plaza de Mayo today. Among a crowd of thousands of people was a group of 20 or 30 youths doing the fascist salute, shouting: Viva España, los judíos: abajo [Down with the Jews]. *The crowd stepped away and started shouting at them to lower their arms. They insisted that it was a national holiday, that there should be no divisions. Other chants one heard included*: Viva la revolución de Mayo; viva la próxima revolución [*Long Live the May Revolution; Long live the next revolution*].

'As I was saying, what is comparable is the sense of filial duty. She voluntarily went to Theresienstadt in search of her blind mother, who she then followed to Auschwitz and would have ended up in the gas chambers if a Nazi (Mengele himself according to her slightly dubious account) hadn't broken her jaw with his foot.'

'If you think that looking after your parents is a filial duty then you clearly live at a time when filial responsibilities are negligible.'

'Maybe. But you didn't seem all that convinced yourself, which is why you had to resort to specious reasoning to keep from killing yourself.'

'The meaning of life can't be ending it and with it all possibility of meaning. You might never discover the meaning of life or it might be that it doesn't exist, but what certainly isn't the answer is the removal of the physical means of asking the question.'

'No argument here. But I can't help but think that it's rather obvious to say that killing oneself can't be the answer to the question of why one shouldn't kill oneself.'

'The idea is that when you don't find a reason to be something, at least you know that not being, an almost instinctive response brought on by desperation, can't be the answer.'

'I shall take that as a piece of grandfatherly advice. In fact, it might even serve in less melodramatic situations. For example, when I translate your diary and am faced with a phrase with no obvious solution, I now know that leaving it untranslated is never the answer.'

'Well, there I don't know if I entirely agree. For example, the phrase '*lesen in Brot und Wein*', which you've just translated as 'reading with bread and wine', I think might have been better left between quotation marks.'

' . . . ?'

'You've never heard of the poem 'Bread and Wine' by Hölderlin?'

'No, actually I haven't, just the football chant: 'Bread and wine, bread and wine . . .' Also there aren't any quotation marks.'

'It's a private diary written in haste, my dear boy. The 'in' refers to a book. Otherwise it sounds like I'm reading while sitting atop of a pile of food . . .'

'Just the same, the unanswered question is whether you found a resolution to your dilemma or not. Because deep down you knew that the meaning of your life was, or is, to be found in study and books.'

'But I'm talking about transcendent, universal meaning.'

'Why can't that coincide with a personal, selfish one? A book is an ambiguous object, it belongs to both realms—the mundane and the spiritual. It's a thing among things but also contains the universe.'

'Books are the only image of God that Jews are allowed to worship. No sculptures or icons. I like that.'

'So being forced to give up your books was like killing yourself. You'd found the meaning of life in them and now you were denied from continuing the experience. That's awful.'

'Your grandmother suffered much worse.'

'But reading that entry in your diary, I find it easier to understand Nazi cruelty than listening to the much more horrifying tale of Grandma Ella.'

'Certainly, the rational, spiritual debacle of Nazism transcends purely physical horror. It's as though their rise removed all possibility of transcendent meaning in life and humanity even after the corporeal devastation had ended. But the persecution and the camps also helped one to find that meaning close by, as can be seen in the following entries from my diary, which with your permission, I shall cite here in your rather flawed translation:

16th April 1936

One would like to get ahead. But there isn't a specific, well-defined objective in view. One would like to study and gain knowledge. Studying brings joy and the acquisition of knowledge would seem to offer good reason to be proud. But that changes quickly, maybe too quickly, into humiliation, contrition and desperation.

22nd November 1936

*Sometimes, yesterday night for instance, when I am sur-
rounded by absolute calm and trying to get to sleep to get
some respite from my everyday obligations, that fearful
but blessed voice, the beloved voice, the only true one,
asks me the question that has always moved me: Why do
you live? Aren't you ruining your inner life? I'm not going
to see [Rabbi] Spier either. Partly because I really don't
have the time, partly because I need to study English and
Spanish, but partly too because I no longer have a real
foundation on which to build the life I had once imagined.*

7th December 1936

*Again and again I am confronted by the question: Is it
worth it? If the question that hung over me before like a
terrible monster was whether there was some meaning to
it, now that question has changed a little. Oddly, one
thinks that they know the answer, or senses it: only relatively speaking of course, from a human perspective. What
is it that God wants with the world? I don't know. But
often when one's health is suffering, when one must make
an effort and break their back, when they are met only
with failure and last but not least when it looks as though
they'll have to work for the rest of their lives, in those
moments when they are not overwhelmed by the 'importance' and pressure of work, the question arises: Is it
worth it? Are all these efforts worth it? Aren't we liable at
any given moment to collapse and close our eyes for eternal rest after thrashing around in nonsensical pursuits?
Does the work make sense?*

25th December 1936

Tonight, at a quarter to twelve, I think, maybe for the first time, that I might have found a solution. A somewhat hazy solution no doubt, but a solution nonetheless. Inside me the urge keeps welling up, telling me that despite everything I should follow my vocation to study philosophy and religion. But the barriers to this are infinite, far greater than me. I never officially graduated secondary school, I'm quite old, there's no money and my parents depend on me. We want, we must, leave Germany. Studying languages is the most important thing. English and Spanish. All the rest is of secondary importance and there's no greater sacrifice I can make than to deprive myself of the time to study philosophy and religion. It is an immense sacrifice that no one else can appreciate. And so the question keeps coming back to me, eating away at me, pressuring and harassing me. And now for the first time I'd like to give myself a gift for all the sacrifice I'm making. I'm going to study, study languages, technical literature about the textile industry, everything, everything with the objective of in a little while, maybe in 17 years [that is, when he turned 40] *earning enough money for me to spend the rest of my life doing things that will be a blessing to me and perhaps a boon to others. I hope that I can achieve this, I hope that I have more energy then than I do today.*

'It's notable that among the infinite number of things that were preventing you from studying, you neglect to mention the fact that you were forbidden from doing so, as you yourself wrote at the beginning of that year.'

'Maybe I'd become so used to the race laws that they didn't count in my mind as an obstacle.'

'Or maybe it was your way of forgetting that you were being persecuted? Other than that entry you never mention the harassment you suffered for being a Jew. It's as though it were a taboo subject even in a private diary.'

'The regime distorted reason to the point that you couldn't even use it as an argument, not even against yourself. To a certain degree, Nazism was just as incomprehensible at the time as it would be for subsequent generations.'

'Still, it's surprising that your only mention of Hitler while you're in Germany is the following anodyne entry from January '37:

Today Adolf Hitler spoke about transforming Berlin into a true capital. The expansion is planned to take 20 years.

'It was a speech he gave to Parliament on the 4-year anniversary of his government coming to power. Maybe the 20-year figure scared me. I was making plans for 17 years in the future and I couldn't imagine the same dictator still being there.'

'Thinking a little more about how you don't mention the issue in your diary, I wonder if the omission isn't a strategy for defence but, rather, a form of attack. Responding to segregation with inclusion, to Judaeophobia with Germanophilia. As though you were saying: *Don't try to convince me that we're different: we both know that we're the same.* Was it possible to be so subtle at the time? Do you have ice in your veins, Grandpa?'

' . . . '

My grandfather won't answer, and it's probably better that way. This isn't a collection of interviews like the one I wrote with my grandmother,[5] it's a novel. I get up from the imaginary chair and leave him alone with the man in the thin shirt whose English was similarly threadbare (and what there was was American). But this nonetheless proved to be ample recompense for Magnus' inadvertent largesse with the coffee.

'Where are you from, if you don't mind me asking?' asked my grandfather in his best Oxford (Dictionary) English.

'I came here from the United States but I was born on the Danube,' stammered the other in an English that has been improved markedly here in both grammar and style by your faithful translator. 'I'm a chess champion, but a fictitious one. Out of a novel by Stefan Zweig, I don't know if you know him?'

'Stefan Zweig? Of course I know him, he's my favourite writer!' Magnus snapped back, almost offended by the question. Having established this, he was able to process the preceding statement. 'Did you say a fictitious champion?'

'Indeed, that's why they don't recognize me. They won't let me play Alekhine.'

Heinz Magnus felt that the coffee, counterintuitively, was making him sleepy. In fact—just as counterintuitively—he felt as though he was slipping into a waking dream. The smoke, the tango music and the gleaming aluminium advertisements for Quilmes beer enhanced this sensation. In fact, the atmosphere rather demanded it. Living in exile had always had a certain

5 *La abuela* (Grandmother), published in German translation under the title *Zwei lange Unterhosen der Marke Hering* (Two Pairs of Hering Trousers)—(enough self-promotion!).

dream-like, or novelistic, quality for Magnus, and, although the feeling had faded in time, it wasn't necessarily because his senses had adapted; there was also the possibility that he'd just come to accept that life was a little unreal.

'What did you say your name was?'

'Oh, right, forgive me: Czentovich. Mirko Czentovich. Thank you very much for the coffee.'

Magnus ran through the names of the different characters in Zweig's novels, trying to determine whether the fantasy life this kid was living had at least some coherence to it, but he couldn't remember any that sounded similar (remember, *Chess Story* would only be published a few years later). He couldn't decide what was more ridiculous, that the boy thought he was a character from a novel or that he'd declared it so openly. He knew that it was always better to admit the truth, and tell it, but he wasn't sure whether this applied to flagrant self-deception or bald-faced lies. Accepting that someone was delusional just because they were sincere about it lent the experience the dangerous air of reality, a weird, dreamy reality perhaps but reality nonetheless. The orchestra started up with a new tune and the audience applauded while my grandfather sat up with a jolt: he'd suddenly had a thought. Although he'd be ashamed to say it out loud; it was evidence of his gradual slide into atheism, he realized that he too, in addition to being his father's son, thought of himself as a character created by God. Of course, he wasn't the only one who felt this way, and that made all the difference in social terms, but deep down, seen from that perspective, his companion's assertion seemed far less absurd, not so different from other *Weltanschauungen* of a similar bent. The distinction, if it existed at all, was analogous to that between legal and illegal drugs, or what we choose to call drugs and what we call medications. If he declared himself to be a member of a people taken from a book, what was the difference between that and this fellow who described himself as having been invented in a different book?

'I too am a character: from the Torah,' he said aloud in a suitably ecumenical tone.

'Do you play chess?' his companion asked, never one to stray from his obsession.

Magnus shook his head but was then suddenly distracted by the arrival of Sonja Graf, who was looking marvellous in spite of her frown. And the fact that she hadn't even looked at him. She was accompanied by the young Estonian Ilmar Raud, about whom we know nothing except that he too would stay in Argentina after the tournament. But he didn't know that yet: it wasn't what he was planning. He was so unprepared for said twist of fate that only a couple of years later, after trying to earn a living playing for cash and giving lessons, he'd die of typhus in the street. Or perhaps in a mental asylum. Some say that he died of starvation, as hard as that may be to believe in a country where instead of saying one 'earns their bread', they say they 'earn their stew', a much more complete meal, as the man at the next table, Najdorf, would note later on in his memoir, explaining his decision to stay in the country after losing his entire family, of 300 members, to the Nazi genocide.

'No chance,' Graf announced, lighting her cigarette. 'Not even under a flag that says "Free", like mine.'

'Yours?' Heinz interjected with a smile, proud and excited that his drawing had been adopted. The boost made him think that his drawing for the bookplate wasn't so bad after all. He'd send it to the printer the very next day.

Only then did Graf recognize the Jewish man from the barber shop. She deigned to nod curtly in his direction before turning back to Czentovich.

'We'll come up with something,' said the bearer of bad news consolingly. 'A talent like yours can't be kept out of this tournament.'

Just then the friendly waiter made his inevitable appearance, and, although Heinz would now have been more than willing to buy a round, for the lady's benefit of course, he had to forbear from doing anything that might cut into the 5-peso raise he'd managed to secure for the following month. His joy at finding his chess player had been undermined by seeing her in the company of another man. He was just as young as Magnus and actually looked quite similar, although he reflected that this might actually be a good sign. Sonja, in contrast, seemed to be thrilled to be surrounded by young men, and in her enthusiasm ordered a round of cognac even though she had barely any more money than Raud, undoubtedly the poorest person at the table. The only solvent one was Czentovich and he'd never bought a round for anyone. Perhaps his money was fictitious too, or at least lacked value in the real world.

'He could play in my place,' Raud suggested.

'Now there's an idea!' Sonja responded gleefully.

Raud was playing black against the Cuban player Alberto López Arce and his game had been suspended until the following day, with the next move placed in a sealed envelope. His offer arose from the fact he didn't think he was in a good position and was going to lose (but he was wrong, he'd win the following day).

'You could try the trick with the Turk,' my grandfather said, continuing to practice his English. 'Maelzel's Turk, the automaton Poe wrote about . . . '

It was almost everything Heinz knew about chess, so he was amazed to find that the chess players had no idea what he was talking about. It's just this kind of contradiction that defines erudition on the one hand and ignorance on the other, if they're not actually on the same branch of the family tree, that is. With great pleasure (he liked to summarize the plot of books almost as much as he did reading them out loud, not to mention the fact that it allowed him to show off in front the woman of his dreams, or at least the best that reality had to offer at the time), Magnus gave them the gist of Edgar Allen Poe's essay in which he exposes the chess-playing robot created by the Hungarian Baron Von Kempelen in the eighteenth century as a fraud. By then it had fallen into the hands of one Maelzel, who toured the principal cities of the United States with his so-called automaton, which beat most (but not all) comers.

Poe had gone to several of these shows, which he then described in great detail so as to explain precisely how the hoax was perpetrated. Magnus couldn't remember all the arguments that Poe had employed to show that the machine was in fact a human and how the little person moved the Turk's arm, just the main points of the debunking, which included its imperfect score:

The Automaton does not invariably win the game. Were the machine a pure machine this would not be the case— it would always win. The 'principle' being discovered by which a machine can be made to 'play' a game of chess, an extension of the same principle would enable it to win a game—a farther extension would enable it to win 'all' games—that is, to beat any possible game of an antagonist. A little consideration will convince anyone that the difficulty of making a machine beat all games, is not in the least degree greater, as regards the principle of the operations necessary, than that of making it beat a single game. If then we regard the Chess Player as a machine, we must suppose (what is highly improbable) that its inventor preferred leaving it incomplete to perfecting it.

Although Heinz wasn't entirely convinced by this argument, he remembered it for a reason and reproduced it now before explaining that Poe had scandalously underestimated the maths. As he'd read in a footnote to the text (he didn't mention that part), Poe's failed theory was similar to that of the Indian raja who ingenuously agreed—as one of the most celebrated founding legends of the game had it—to pay the reward requested by its inventor of a grain for the first square and for this to progressively double with each of the following squares on the board, ending up with a sum as exorbitant as the number of possible moves, which was incalculable even for machines that had not yet been invented.

But Heinz cared less about Poe's mathematical accuracy than his brave quest for the truth, which he saw as similar to that of Palaephatus, a disciple of Aristotle who set himself the pointless task of using the weapons of logic—what today (and in 1939) we would call taking a 'scientific' approach—to debunk the Greek myths. The two quixotic writers were united across epochs and geography by their need to use all that rhetorical heavy artillery to undermine something that was going to collapse under its own weight anyway. However, Magnus went on, the automaton issue—what today (not in 1939) we would call 'artificial intelligence'—had already been addressed by Leibniz so it was something that nonetheless should concern all those interested in the possibilities and limitations of science, even if the purpose was solely to expose hoaxes.

This brief speech impressed his diminutive audience, and if it had been addressed to more important figures—like those at the neighbouring table—it would almost certainly still be around today (in a book called *Magnus by Magnus*). Once again, the first person to react was Sonja Graf, who at least knew who Poe was, albeit not as a chess historian but, rather, as a writer of mysteries and a critic of a game, whose 'elaborate frivolity' he rated somewhere below whist. Perhaps for that very reason, Sonja was inclined to believe that the Turk was another made-up story, a mystery in which no one died, they were just defeated. She didn't hesitate to share her opinion that it sounded a little too simplistic and unlikely. Magnus was forced to insist in alarm that it really was true, or rather it was true that it wasn't an automaton, or rather . . . Poe had gone to all that effort to debunk a fiction and now he found himself being forced to prove that it had actually happened! Magnus reminded them that *Robinson Crusoe* had initially been read as a factual account rather than a novel, but this reference had no effect. In his frustration, he ended up resorting to a strange argument worthy of Palaephatus himself: if the Turk had been fictitious, then Czentovich must know him. He immediately realized that this was an absurd assumption, even in their realm of ironic rationalism: it was like asking Ilmar Raud if he knew an Estonian just because they came from the same country.

'Will there ever exist a machine that can beat a man at chess?' Raud asked, redirecting the conversation to territory that was equally inscrutable to all.

'If we can make living machines that are half as effective as the death-dealing ones we've already made, there's no doubt about it,' Graf said, showing that her faith in the possibilities of science was as great as the flaws of humanity.

'The question is whether, if the robot was created by man, it would still be a human achievement,' Magnus interjected.

'That's true,' Graf said, giving him a sideways glance that Heinz felt was in itself full of possibilities. 'It would have to be a robot built by a robot.'

Encouraged by the cognac, or the fact that he hadn't had to pay for it, Czentovich related that at the universal exposition in New York, an event easily overlooked (in 1939 certainly, not so much today), he'd seen an enormous golden robot that was operated by telephone, spoke in a metallic voice and even smoked cigarettes. He couldn't remember what the marvel had been called (and certainly not the fact that it had been built to promote a brand of domestic appliances, showing that even back then advertising was a scam perpetrated not against the consumers but the manufacturers persuaded to pay for it); he couldn't remember its name (and we're not about to give it free advertising here), but he did recall that it had been presented as a 'Friendly Frankenstein', a choice that overlooked the fact that Frankenstein's monster had also been friendly at first, or that it had at least been built with the best of intentions. Not to mention the fact that Frankenstein was the inventor, not the monster.

'The chess-playing robot is only a matter of time,' Czentovich concluded in support of Poe's thesis. 'When it comes, we'll be more obsolete than gaslighters.'

'You might say that electricity is the robot that will eventually invent the robot that will electronically checkmate us,' Raud concluded.

'Talking about mate, have you tried mate?' Magnus asked for no apparent reason, just to contradict my assertions about his failure to adapt to Argentina, I suppose. 'They say that it removes your appetite, but it just makes me sleepy.'

'What amazes me about this country is how everyone goes around saying "check" all the time. I keep thinking that they're talking to me,' Graf joked.

'It's not "check", it's "che". It's what they say to get each other's attention.'

'Che-players, the lot of them.'

They all laughed at the bad joke: it was the prerogative of the person picking up the bill, and she was so pleased that she paid for another round. My grandfather checked the time on his pocket watch—I have it in a drawer somewhere (stuck on a quarter to three exactly, I'd always assumed in the afternoon, but now I'm not so sure)—and let out a gigantic yawn that verged on rudeness even though he covered his mouth. Today was, for his life in Argentina, what this chapter is to this book, and although he was tempted by the idea of letting it stretch on into the following one, in company perhaps, he decided to pay his share and leave.

'Can I walk you to the hotel?' he ventured hopefully to Sonja.

'I think I'd rather stay a little longer,' she replied, although she actually did want to leave.

'I didn't mean right now,' Magnus replied, although he had said that.

'In that case, with pleasure,' Graf said happily.

But a few minutes later, discouraged by her reply, Magnus paid and left. The move caught Sonja Graf off guard, but not in a bad way.

10

BETWEEN LIVING FICTIONS

In his *Brief and Extraordinary Tales*, Borges describes a game of chess played by two kings that will determine the fate of the battle being fought by their armies.

By nightfall—'The Shadow of the Moves', based on the Welsh legend of Mabinogion, concludes—*one of the kings tipped over the board. He'd been checkmated. Shortly afterwards a rider covered in blood arrived to tell him*: *Your army flees, your kingdom is lost.*

Similarly, the Tournament of Nations, if it makes any sense to compare legends with reality, embarked upon the decisive classifying round just as Europe was embarking upon the decisive stage of the prelude to the Second World War. Here in Argentina, everything was shaping up for Germany to confront Poland (both teams were top of their respective groups and would then compete for first place in the tournament, which would eventually go to Germany by half a point); two countries heading towards a final showdown. In Europe, the teams were positioning their pieces with more or less the same goal in mind.

Hitler had sent his ultimatum to Poland: either the country voluntarily allowed Germany to annex the territory it wanted as Austria and Czechoslovakia had already done or the Nazi army would take it by force. For the troubled recipient, it was like a fraudulent declaration of check, or at least one they refused to accept because some of the previous moves had been illegal, or because the rules of the game themselves were flawed. Even if they surrendered the piece in question, the equivalent of a queen, to protect the remaining ones, they knew, like every player under severe pressure, that the disproportionate sacrifice was just a delaying tactic to gain a little time. Winning the game was out of the question. In fact, the Nazi–Soviet Pact that had been announced a few days before had already agreed that the Russians would get the rest of the country, although this was yet to become public knowledge.

But it would be a mistake to think that the position was clear. They never are when you look at them more closely, forgetting for a moment that we know what the next move was and even how the match ended. This course was perhaps plotted in bolder lines than other potential options, but the thousands of alternative paths abandoned to the limbo of possibility explain why it turned out to be the one chosen. The problem was the pieces seemingly destined to play minor roles. Italy, for example. The Russo-German pact had apparently to put an end to the Italo-German anti-communist pact, leaving Mussolini free to take the side of Poland along with France and Great Britain. This strategy—offensive like all the best defences—might easily have been dubbed with an Italian name as it was very similar to what Italy had done in the First World War, betraying its Teutonic ally after feeling betrayed by them.

By now the reader might be thinking that the chess metaphor has been stretched to its absolute limit: on the board, the pieces can't decide to change colour and attack their former comrades. But what can happen in chess is for one of your pieces to become more of a liability to you than your opponent, or for your strategy to be turned into a trap by an unexpected move, one that was only made effective by the path you chose. So in fact it is perfectly possible for a piece to change shades. The first to see this is the analyst: to them, each side is both familiar and alien at the same time.

Everyone becomes an analyst the moment they start to study a position as though the game were still being played; one of the magical qualities of chess is that the measurement of time is an intrinsic part of it, as the linguist Ferdinand de Saussure noted when comparing it to the system of symbols in a language at any given moment. The equivalent of the analysts who gathered in the first-floor foyer of the Politeama Theatre to discuss the games being reproduced on the YPF wall charts would be the editorials in the newspapers written by civilians who thought they knew more about the game than the generals, although of course they didn't have the least influence on how it was fought. Mario Mariani, for example, an Italian writer and columnist who wrote 'exclusively' for *Crítica*, in his column of 18th August, actually made use of a chess metaphor to explain the situation in Europe, going on to speculate that Hitler might give up on invading Poland and form an alliance with France and Great Britain to take control of Italy and thus have a 'door to the Mediterranean'.

As we know, this move remained in the limbo (or hell) of possibility. To quote a headline from the same newspaper, 'The Situation is Rife with Confusionism'. The press made a sizeable contribution to said chaos, with *Crítica* at the fore. When the war broke out, the newspaper of Botana (and Yanofsky) announced that Berlin, according to a cable dated the 1st of September, had been bombed by Polish warplanes. It wasn't the craziest piece of news to come out at the time:

PURE ARYAN NAZIS APPEAL TO THE JEWS FOR HELP,
OFFERING AMNESTY IN RETURN FOR TAKING UP
ARMS ON BEHALF OF GERMANY

News from Berlin almost as surprising as the Nazi–Soviet Pact. A brief item that in these days of international turbulence and the lead-up to war might easily go unnoticed by newspaper editors. And yet it is of enormous importance to the hundred thousand Jews spread around the world, exiles who have fled Nazi persecution.

'They can come back to their homeland if they want'; they will be well treated, especially those in a fit state to take up arms. They will be immediately incorporated into the glorious German army and will enjoy the great honour of dying for the killers of their fathers and brothers. Italian anti-fascists and Jews are certain that, if the danger increases, Mussolini will make the same offer: he will solemnly declare that he knows only Italians, that all domestic rifts are forgotten and that the most important duty is to defend the fatherland.

Two things always go together: cowardice and cruelty. A cruel person is always a coward and a coward is always cruel. The brown shirts who dragged old beggars through the streets of Berlin cackling and crushing their skulls on the tramlines just because they weren't pure Aryans today appeal desperately to survivors of the anti-Semitic butchery and pogroms to hurry up and enlist under the flag of those who tortured their race—their murderers.

Such is the racial pride of pure Aryans! They might well be Aryan but there's nothing pure about people like that: not their blood, their souls or their minds.

A wonderful show of cowardice! After their unprece-dented displays of cruelty. But an even greater show of cowardice will follow, a cowardice we don't want to nor can even imagine—the cowardice of the liberals, democrats, socialists and communists who answer the call to arms and go to shed the blood the tyrants have left them, to save their state of tyranny.

The columns of the newspaper's star chess analyst, Raúl Capablanca, were just as erratic. Once the Hamilton Russel Cup had begun, he announced that the final would be between Sweden and Argentina, neither of whom would even come in the top three. And just as *Crítica*'s reporting was guided by its interests or at least its political desires (to see the fall of Hitler), Capablanca's commentary was patently designed to curry favour with local authorities in the hope that they would organize his long-awaited rematch with Alekhine.

But other things really did happen. Even when a game looks to all intents and purposes to be over, there is the possibility of a move that doesn't appear to make sense, or that seeks to delay the inevitable. Poland could have given in, as we said (and as Austria and Czechoslovakia already had) and thus an armed conflict with incalculable consequences (a grain squared) might have been avoided. This faith in a kind of agreed draw to keep world peace lingered on even after that fateful 1st of September, as can be seen in the *Private Bulletin* (international edition):

1st September 1939

Today, at five in the morning, Germany started to bomb Poland. But still I think that the situation might be resolved. (Here, for 'resolved', my grandfather uses the verb *arreglieren*, which doesn't exist in German except in that godawful dialect that came to be known as Belgrano German because of the number of German emigrants who lived in that area of Buenos Aires. The basic rule for this local jargon was to take a word in Spanish and give it a Teutonic twist. Which is in fact what German, pure German, did with many Latin words when it added them to its elegant vocabulary. A vocabulary so elegant that even if one did start using non-existent terms like *arreglieren*, they were very unlikely to be corrected for fear of coming off as *burren*.)

2nd September 1939

This morning we gave up all hope of a peaceful solution. This afternoon we think we see a thin ray of hope.

3rd September 1939

Today, at six this morning local time, the inevitable happened. Britain has declared war on Germany. Shortly afterwards, France too declared war on Germany. Let's hope that they'll soon be cracking that criminal's head open.

But the sirens that would ring early that September morning to announce the official commencement of a conflict with terrible consequences haven't gone off just yet, not even in its chess-based metaphor. Getting back to that late night, a move that shouldn't bother anyone (we've been hopping back and forth the whole time, everything recounted here is history and thus already done and dusted, in that sense we can rest easy, or succumb to the worst kind of despair), the early morning of 31st August, we find ourselves in the lead-up to another catastrophe, in this case a domestic one; a very appropriate topic for a novel, even the kind where you know the ending in advance.

Heinz Magnus had come to the conclusion that to get some time alone with Sonja he'd have to take her out of her comfort zone: not just the realm of chess, but also that of men. When he found out that she was free that night (so free twice over), he decided to invite her to the movies. He'd looked through the listings in search of something appropriate for the occasion, maybe something made in Argentina so he could whisper the translation into her ear, but ended up choosing an excellent European one: *La Bête Humaine* by Jean Renoir. It almost certainly wasn't a romance but there was no reason to believe that they were the only kind of film that single women liked. In fact, the assumption would be rather condescending. She was a boyish chess player with a sharp tongue; she'd probably take offence if he tried to take her to a cheap melodrama. She wasn't a housewife, she was a woman of the world, an intellectual. Actually, to treat her in any other way would be to do himself down too: he would have taken offence if she'd turned out to want to watch such cheap rubbish. And while these were little more than excuses to watch the film of his choosing, there was nothing wrong with that. At the end of the day, Heinz didn't want Sonja to be interested in the movie, but him. This was a choice designed to achieve just that.

So, that Wednesday he went out on his lunch break, headed for the Ambassador Cinema on Calle Lavalle and bought a pair of tickets for the 9.15 show. After work, he went straight to the hotel where he'd learnt the German woman was staying. To avoid having to explain himself, he asked for her at the reception desk, exaggerating his accent (which made him sound more French than anything). Just as he'd feared, and, in fact, expected, Miss Graf wasn't in at the time but if the gentleman liked he could leave a message. This was exactly what he had planned for, so he shuffled away and pretended to write a note he'd already got ready in his pocket: a ticket 'For the bearded lady' to the movies 'in the company of her colleague, the ringmaster'. This cryptic reference to their supremely promising first meeting seemed particularly appropriate. Certain that he'd find her waiting at the Ambassador at the appointed hour, he went home to change and freshen up.

But the bearded lady had other plans that night. Or rather the plan was to be spontaneous. Days off always took her by surprise. They were the only move she never anticipated, as she used to say. She was sure she wouldn't go to Harrods, especially not with Vera Menchik de Stevenson, who hadn't said a word to her since the competition had begun. Was she afraid of her? It was possible. Although the champion was unbeaten while Sonja had suffered a painful loss to the Russo-American Mona Mary Karff (with whom, to make things worse, she was sharing a room at the hotel), she felt stronger than ever and her potential opponent must have got wind of this. Great champions pretend not to be interested in the rest of the field, looking down on everyone from an ivory tower of triumph, surrounded by an entourage that protects them from potential rivals. And yet they live in fear of losing everything they've won, like kings and their treasure. Being the second best was, in that regard, an advantage, an infinite luxury which she'd have liked to hold onto even if she did beat the champion. But nobody gets to be second without wanting to be first. It's the first (and second) law of all competitive sport.

Partly because she didn't really know what to do with her free time in this rural megalopolis (you saw more animals on the street than you did in German villages. Even the striking sight of dairy cows delivering their produce fresh—and warm—from door to door) and partly because she wanted to shake off the bitterness of the previous night's defeat as soon as possible, Graf was relieved to hear from the organizing committee that there had been a scheduling mix-up and that she actually did have to play that night. So she sat down with particular enthusiasm to face the Canadian player Annabelle Louhgeed-Freedman who was playing her first chess Olympiad. With our privileged knowledge, we can reveal that Louhgeed-Freedman would win just a single game and come last. So, of course, Graf destroyed her. It only took her 33 moves, and none of them taxed her mind overly. When she stood up from her chair, it was quarter past ten at night. There hadn't been a scheduling mix-up; the organizers had just got ahead of themselves: the woman who played under the banner of freedom was indeed free for the evening.

At lunch, she'd heard that that night there would be a living chess show somewhere in the centre. She asked how to get there and walked unescorted (not that anyone noticed; she both dressed and walked like a man). As unlikely as it sounds for a professional, Graf had never been to one of these shows, not even during her brief stay in Ströbeck, the German town that had been dedicated exclusively to chess since medieval times and where living chess was played in public squares whenever the weather allowed. Sonja had a dream that she would never share with anyone: people had a habit of interpreting dreams without anyone asking them to, hence the success of psychoanalysis. Graf had a childhood wish, which remained with her through adulthood because the nature of childish wishes is that they don't evolve but remain inviolate, intact year after year, increasing exponentially in power. Again, not unlike the famous grains of corn on the chessboard. Susann had long yearned not only to attend one of these shows but also to take an active part in them, as a bishop if she were given the choice. The King's Bishop, so as to be close to her favourite piece when she was a child:

> *When I was very little, very young, I boasted the virtues of mischievousness, disobedience and cheek—*we read in *This is How a Woman Plays—in truth, I still answer to all of these qualities. When I turned 12 or 14, I fell head over heels in love. There's nothing so out of the ordinary about that, it must happen to every girl. They encounter their idea of perfection and swoon over their dashing prince.*
>
> *But my love took a different form and it will surely come as a surprise to you, my dear reader* [or my dear reader] *to learn of my object of affection: a King, a King of wood. Svelte and enigmatic, thoughtful and melancholy, the King of the noblest, most spiritual of games, the King of Chess. He occupied all my thoughts and fantasies and I was only happy when I could be with him, confiding my hopes and dreams to him.*
>
> *Many a time did I reject the dolls and toys given to me by my parents and friends, choosing instead to spend my*

time alone: some of the happiest moments of my child-
hood. I cried so hard when, playing against a friend or sib-
ling, we were forced to lay down our arms at the feet of
the enemy. As I cried I would beg forgiveness for my care-
lessness, solemnly promising not to leave him so exposed
ever again.

    He would always understand completely, I was certain
of it, and sharing that pure feeling of mine helped me in
the future. My character developed in the glow of this
great love.

Although today she'd have preferred to have fallen in love with a
pawn, or the bishop itself, at least Sonja could reassure herself
that she'd never wanted to be the queen, a fetish common among
female chess players when they're not much larger than the pieces
with which they identify.

Driven, then, by this secret yearning, Sonja walked down Calle
Corrientes, which was brighter than any found in the City of
Light, rounded the Obelisk of Defeat, as she'd named it in echo
of the Arc de Triomphe in Paris (associating them with their rather
obvious genital counterparts) and eventually got to Luna Park
Stadium. She had to walk around almost the entire building before
finding the entrance to home of basketball, wrestling, ice skating
and boxing, to judge from the plaster figures at each corner. She
liked the idea of chess taking its place among these sports, especially the latter for which she felt a strange attraction that had
never been satisfied, in this case due to feminine modesty. She paid
the general entrance fee, which cost the same as tickets to see her
play; she couldn't decide whether they were overly cheap or expen-
sive, and found herself in a hall with an enormous chessboard

at least 10 metres across, on which men and women in fairly simple, rather amateurish costumes, the kind one might see at an end-of-year school play, were moving around. The most pathetic character was undoubtedly the black king (the only kind that might attract a white girl). He was shorter than the opposing pawns and they were hardly tall themselves (strangely, the tallest actor played one of the white pawns). This disappointed her to the point of girlish tears. And indeed, there seemed to be a lot of little girls in the audience for an evening show in the middle of the week. The only thing that kept her from leaving immediately was her shame at the tears pricking her eyes. The other thing keeping her there was the fact that they were reproducing one of the most entertaining games from the tournament so far: Alekhine's Panov attack against Eliskases' Caro-Kann defence. Two men in black suits gestured solemnly as they provided commentary from the centre of the stage, walking among the pieces as though they were choreographers: it was Eliskases and Alekhine in person (the player moving the pieces was a piece himself!) Although she didn't understand what they were saying, it reassured her to know that in spite of their lengthy explanations and gestures, no one else in the audience did either. However, they listened attentively and respectfully, similarly to the audience that had come to watch her and the other players at the Politeama Theatre. Perhaps this living audience was also part of the show, she thought, an idea that led her to hope that the following day, when she was playing again, she would feel one with the board. Deep down, she was forever trying to recover the uninhibited feelings she'd experienced when she'd first started to play. It was the first thing she'd lost when she turned professional. This is true of all artists: they feel a part of their early works, but then, when they begin to see them for what they are, that's when they start to slip away.

But she wouldn't have to wait long to feel like a little girl again, or at least to have an opportunity to feel that way. When the pieces broke ranks and started to dance to music played by an equally live orchestra, a sight that she found deeply disturbing, (ordinarily she hated studying games but she'd been engrossed in this one, it was like a radio play), she decided to leave. During the musical interlude, she had a coffee in the foyer cafe, which is where she came across J. Yanofsky, who was heading in the other direction.

'The free player!' he exclaimed, immediately recognizing the German woman with the boy's haircut.

The phrase was clearly a double entendre, Graf noticed, and she enjoyed the cheek. She also liked the fact that the man had recognized her as though she was a film star, a career path she'd hadn't wholly given up on, and that he spoke the Jewish variant of German that she so enjoyed. But most of all she liked the man; a scruffy, pudgy 40-something who exuded virility, especially in comparison to the rather feminine look of most of the locals.

'I'll pay, order whatever you like,' he continued in a Yiddish that welled up from deep inside him, especially once he'd got going. It was the language in which his mother had raised him when he was a little boy and was now the only thing he had left of her. 'Tonight, I'm the ringmaster. If you like, I can have them play one of your games. I could even put you on stage. It would be wonderful: the player as a piece from her own game. Which would you like to be?'

The suggestion in general, but especially the final question, once again had her on the brink of tears. This man must have read her mind! And then he appeared to read it again when he interpreted her reluctant silence as being that of an adult presented with the chance of realizing a childhood dream that could only disappoint her, making her feel worse than if she let the opportunity pass. Correctly seeing that a wish is a wish and that realizing it would be a mortal error, the apparently un-Argentine man filled the silence with a blurted explanation of how he'd conceived the event, which was sponsored by the newspaper where he worked, who he was representing that night, just as he had been on the night at the Politeama when he'd seen her play.

Of all the information and stories that he managed to squeeze into just a few minutes, what most struck Graf, or at least what she understood best from the man's hurried, broken stream— his words tripped over one another as though he were constantly trying to make up for a previous mistake—was related to children. This explained the significant underage presence in the stadium. It seemed that it had been his idea to explicitly market the event as being suitable for children, appealing to parents with the irresistible slogan: 'Bring your child and give them a memory that will last a lifetime.'

'People always talk about their inner child, but they forget the adult inside every child,' Yanofsky went on, still in Yiddish. 'Little adults don't want to learn about things that will be useful to them, they want to enjoy experiences appropriate for their age—that is, inappropriate for their level of physical development. If you think about it, you'll note that the best memories we have, for better or worse, are of things that came too early, or that seemed out of place. They were meant for other people but we got in the way, so to speak. They're stolen memories, they belong to someone else.

Let me give you a personal example, although I'm sure you have your own. When I was very young, my father took me to see a boxing match. As we set out, he said to me: "You're very young for this but I wanted to show you so you'll remember it properly." It was the only thing my father ever gave me, in addition to a half-brother I met a few days ago.'

After briefly going through her own memories of childhood, which she would later make impersonal in *I am Susann* (and she certainly is Susann), Sonja realized that what she remembered with the greatest intensity was sexual experiences inappropriate for her age. And not just the unpleasant ones like the incident that had got her locked up in the reformatory for girls (where she had discovered the delights of Sappho, showing that even Hell has its bright side). She also had amusing memories of inappropriate sexual advances:

> *On that street was a shop of expensive, alluring perfumes where the owner attended his young customers as attentively as he could. He was always giving Susann large jars of scent that she would then give out to her brothers and sisters, who greatly enjoyed the gifts. Of course, as the years went by and the girl's body developed, the perfumier's subconscious male desires were inflamed and he was no longer satisfied with just giving out gifts. Occasionally, as they happily chatted away he'd suddenly say:*
>
> *'Tell me, do you need money?'*
>
> *'What a question, of course I do!'*
>
> *'Well, if you kiss me, I'll give you 20 pesos.'*

'You can't put "pesos" in an anecdote that occurs in Germany in the 30s. I say that translator to translator, with the greatest respect.'

'But it's easier to understand.'

'"Marks" paints a much clearer picture.'

'No, because people won't know how much it is.'

'And how much is that in pesos?'

'Quite a lot.'

'Well, if you're going to Argentinize everything, put Susana instead of Susann and stop using so many adverbs, it'll devalue them, just like the peso.'

'I'll bear that in mind, thanks for your suggestion.'

'Thanks? That'll be 20,000 australes, please.'

How odd, Susann thought. So men make a business out of even the most intimate things. What a strange world! It was a sizeable sum; but still the girl laughed brazenly in the man's face and stepped back, away from him. After that, every time the man saw her, he repeated his offer more insistently, so desperate was he to kiss Susann's lips.

The girl related the perfumier's outrageous proposition to her brothers and—of course—the four boys persuaded her to take the money but to renege on the deal.

'OK, but how do I get out of it?'

'Easy! We'll be standing outside the door and when you give the word, we'll rush in to save you.'

And that's what they did. The girl went to the shop with a beatifically innocent expression on her face, and immediately broached the man's favourite subject.

'I'll give you whatever you want to kiss your lips, to feel your kisses.'

'Really?' she asked. 'How much would you give me . . . ?'

The monster came over brandishing a 50-peso note. Susann almost fainted; she'd never seen so much money. She thought about all the nice things she could buy with it and decided to play the situation diplomatically.

'Give it to me,' she said calmly. 'And then I'll give you a kiss.'

The aroused man, blind with desire, put the note in the girl's hand and leant in to collect his reward. But Susann let out a furious scream and the door opened to reveal four horrifying faces staring threateningly at the shop owner. Bewildered, he was forced to dissemble his twisted game and the girl slipped silently away.

The young siblings shared the money between them with glee. The matter appeared to be settled but there's a reason that people say there's no cure for love. The poor man was so determined to kiss the girl's lips that many more pesos—marks—passed through Susann's hands.

'Do you have children?' Graf asked, ostensibly sticking with the theme but, of course, really asking something else.

'My God!' Yanofsky exclaimed with a frown, pretending to be offended, perhaps a little too convincingly. 'Do I look that old?'

'No, well, it's . . .' a man had never made her stammer before, except for the judge when she'd had to testify in the incest case, and her tyrannical father. So: never in a good way.

'Well, you certainly don't, do you?'

Although the compliment was direct, there was still something sweet about it. The man had the air of a boxer. His punches were heavy but polished; professional.

'I wish my father had taken me to see a boxing match,' Sonja said, given they were apparently indulging in nostalgia. 'But he never let me out anywhere, not even to play chess.'

Yanofsky put down his half-finished glass, checked his pocket watch and without saying a word ducked and weaved a little, inviting her to come with him like a boxer leading his opponent into the corner of the ring. Outside, they got into a taxi and headed for the Avellaneda Sports Club where several amateur boxers Yanofsky had already had his eye on would be pitting their skills against each other.

11

DOING BATTLE SIMULTANEOUSLY

Of the 928 games played at the Tournament of Nations, 84 fewer than the planned 1012, the reasons for the shortfall are discussed here, although they'll be familiar to anyone with even a passing knowledge of the subject: among all the matches at the ill-fated Olympiad which almost never took place at all for financial reasons, the racist joke levelled against Yanofsky in Chapter Eight being quite accurate (because the government hadn't transferred the assigned funds, a call went out for donations of tables and pieces in exchange for their having possibly been used by grandmasters before they were returned); of the meagre under a thousand, poorly financed matches, that of the German Elfriede Rinder against the American Mona May Karff on the night of 30th August was not particularly remarkable, not for specialists or the general public. But it contained within it a secret still unknown even to expert (but less poetic) historians that shall now be revealed exclusively to readers of this novel.

To the American of Russian origin (who had spent her early years in Palestine) the game against the German of German origin (who had always lived in Germany) had a special spice to it. First, because they were rivals for the only position still available, behind Menchik and Graf, or vice versa (although third place

CHESS WITH MY GRANDFATHER

would in fact go to a surprise contender: the Chilean player Belen Carrasco); and second, because one of them was Jewish (or vice versa). In any case, there were at least two reasons not to lose to the German: it was a matter of both sporting and racial honour.

The game began as usual at 9.30 p.m. 'on the dot', as Argentinians tend to describe anything that happens within 20 minutes of the appointed hour. At the sound of the gong that marked the beginning and end of each day, giving the occasion an Oriental air in lieu of any actual Asian participation (although there'd be plenty of that in the 'real metaphor', or war), the German began with e4 and Karff answered with the similarly classic Sicilian defence (d4), leading to an Indian attack on the king named not for indigenous Americans but the original Indians, from India.

Rinder's choice was less a strategy than a secretive wink or nod in the hopes of sealing a secret pact. By going through the classic moves of this opening, she was citing another game, that between Samuel Rosenthal vs Gustav Richard Neumann in the middle of the previous century, in Paris. Making a direct reference to a Jew under the current circumstances was more than a *captatio benevolentiae* expressing her disgust with what her government was doing to her opponent's race. The German's intention was to affirm her sympathies with the game's result. As she was unable to say this out loud and letting her opponent win would have been too obvious, not to mention the fact that the gesture might have been taken as condescending rather than friendly (they say that the best defence is a good offence but forget that there is no greater offence than a deliberate defeat), it occurred to Rinder that citing a match played long ago might be a good way of reaching her opponent and, in the process, sending a message to the world. At the end of the day, chess players don't speak in German, English or Hebrew, they speak in chess and although it may be a language of conflict, there's nothing to lose in trying it out for something else. Also, armistices are military in nature; they're articulated in military tone and language.

She had several potential matches in mind, in each of which a Jew played white, all of them ending in a draw, and opted for this one when her opponent replied with the queen's bishop pawn. For the next few moves, she thought they'd reached an understanding even though her opponent didn't replicate Neumann's moves exactly (she saw this as a strategy to avoid suspicion from chess enthusiasts). But her hopes were dashed on the fifth move when Karff, instead of moving her knight to e3, decided to mirror her own *fianchetto* on the king's side before launching an unexpected attack on the opposite flank, forcing Rinder to withdraw a knight she'd placed there in the hopes that the (feigned) struggle would be concentrated on the other side of the board.

Her intention to make a secret arrangement for a draw had failed to get through: her opponent had no inkling of it. Karff was a long way away, mentally speaking. She was detached from the game, as can be seen in the way she left her queen exposed during the unnecessary attack or from her thirteenth move in which she shifted her best piece from d7 to c7 where she'd meant to put it in the first place (still a bad idea, as would soon become evident). These and other mistakes, unheard of in such an important match, would force her to resign by the fortieth move, although the game had been up since the moment her rook was taken. The fact that she didn't resign beforehand wasn't down to stubbornness or fighting spirit but, again, because she wasn't paying proper attention.

The Jewish players had plenty of reasons, which would shortly become inescapable, to be distracted from the tournament. An unfortunately infamous episode would be the match between the Pole Teodor Regedzingski and the Swede Ekenberg Bengt in which the fourth board of the second-placed team would lose a very valuable point—the one that might have won them the championship—because he was forced to play on the same day that the German army bombarded his home city of Lodz.

But this wasn't true of Mona Karff: she and her family lived a long way away from the war zone. How, then, might we explain these blatant mistakes, which would send her down into fifth place, just below Rinder? The answer is simple: because her surname was similar to that of Sonja Graf, at least to the ears of an Argentine concierge.

An hour before the match, the envelope that Heinz Magnus had left for Graf had been accidentally sent to the American woman's room. My grandfather's audacious invitation had distracted her from Rinder's subtle suggestion. What most disturbed her, in addition to not knowing this impudent suitor and not being able to meet the appointment, if only out of curiosity (how could he know that she was divorced?); what most gave her food for thought during the match was the fact that the 'ringmaster' had addressed her as 'the bearded lady'. How did he know that it had been her childhood nickname in honour of her choice of costume at a school party one year? Was he a former schoolmate who'd emigrated to Argentina? One who had perhaps grown up to become a ringmaster?

So, this explains why the intended recipient of the message would never have made the appointment even if she had had the day off and actually enjoyed French cinema (which she hated). The fault in both cases lay in the lap of the suitor. He was doubly to blame: he'd been overly familiar in not putting the recipient's name on the envelope and had also been overly clever, like Rinder, in his choice of venue for their rendezvous. My grandfather read *Crítica* and so must have known that a living chess show was being held that night. It had been heavily advertised in the newspaper over the previous few days and offered an excellent middle ground: it would get Graf a little out of her comfort zone without forcing her too far into his own. But expecting a bipolar person to find middle ground would be poor writing, so I won't chastise myself too much.

And neither did Heinz as he stood in front of the ambassador. He was eventually forced to admit that his plan had failed and started to look for someone to whom he could sell his extra ticket. This was God's will and there was nothing he could do but accept it. In fact, he should be grateful. The woman wasn't for him; asking her out had been a foolish idea. He was too old for crazy flings, he needed to find the mother of his children, he concluded, to the detriment of this novel but very much to the benefit of my father and, by extension, me. What he wanted, as he would write when he met my grandmother Liselotte, was 'the complete housewife', but also someone who was 'very intelligent', a match in which 'we can somehow complete and complement each other.' The bearded lady, in contrast, represented the precise opposite of these ideals. God be praised, Heinz thought, or prayed rather, for having prevented the meeting from taking place.

'Would you like a ticket?' he asked the only person who seemed to be lurking outside the theatre, apparently also waiting for someone whom the Almighty had deemed unworthy.

'Thank you, that's very kind of you,' said the man, taking it as a gift and, as Heinz didn't dare rectify the error, that's what it became.

To demonstrate his gratitude, the man accompanied his benefactor into the theatre and sat next to him. At this point we should explain that the character in question is the same one who a decade ago tried to seduce Silvio Astier in a motel room in the third chapter of Roberto Arlt's *The Mad Toy*, so whoever he had been waiting for, it certainly wasn't a woman. After that bad experience, he desisted from bribing concierges to let him into the rooms of young men in favour of furtive encounters on the street. The cinema (especially French cinema) was always a promising hunting ground. This wouldn't be the case with my grandfather, however, for whom exchanging female company, beard notwithstanding, for a man, as clean-shaven as he might be, would have been a step too far, almost a form of revenge wreaked by the being competing with the Bearded One for control of his life. In any case, he had forgotten his annoyance by the time the newsreel 'Events in Argentina' ended and the film began:

31st August 1939 [Dubbed from the original by the author]

Yesterday I saw the movie La Bête Humaine. First of all: it's one of the greatest, most important and best films of recent years. The photography is unique. For instance, the train journey when they go through the tunnel. The train got closer and closer to the tunnel, then it plunges inside and you can't see a thing: darkness, pitch black. Far in the distance you see a light no bigger than a pinhead; the pinhead grows bigger and bigger until it's full-size: the end of the tunnel through which the train rushes out. Then there was the aspect [the shot] *that one sees of the second inspector in his flat with the windows overlooking the railway. I was especially struck by the photography of the engine, both the wheels and the engine room. And now the characters. The men are good but their blood is poisoned. By the vices of their parents or grandparents. At certain points in their lives they are overwhelmed by sadness and a diabolical need to assuage their pointless and inexplicable rage by killing a man. It must be the profound question of life that moves them so: the whys and wherefores. Their answer is to end a life so that it will disappear from an existence where such an awful question is possible. Once the crime has been committed, their blood cools and they are able to control their spirit again. But it's too late. What they so feared has happened and in the light of day they can't stand the pain their deeds are causing them. They must eliminate another life, but this time their own.*

According to the film and the epigraph from the Emile Zola novel on which it is based, the murderer (or one of them) owes his 'crisis' to his parents' and grandparents' alcoholism. At no point does it say anything about the 'profound question of life that moves them: the whys and wherefores'. Given that the crises suffered by Jacques can't be explained by doctors but include a 'sadness that forces you hide like a beast at the bottom of a hole', I believe that my grandfather was doing what they call 'projecting' (it's cinema, after all) his own fits of depression and suicidal impulses. The emphasis he places on the first scene, which lasts about 30 seconds, is a clear demonstration that he's seeing metaphors rather than images; in this case, the light at the end of the tunnel.

CHESS WITH MY GRANDFATHER

'One of the greatest, most important and best films of recent years,' said Magnus when the lights came up, projecting the woman he'd invited onto the stranger sitting next to him.

'And to think that all this is about to be reduced to rubble,' said his companion, offering him a cigarette, which was refused (a bad sign).

Excited by this sentiment, he tended to say something very similar almost every day (perhaps the All-Knowing had sent this man instead?), Magnus shared his opinion that European culture would be lost for ever if people couldn't be found to protect and cherish it. They agreed that America wasn't up to the task because the only culture they cared about was base and popular, and so it was absolutely critical to gather together, in this European-style city, a group of people determined to salvage what they could. Eventually, they found their way back to the beginning; introducing themselves. The other man was also of European origin: his parents had been born in Russia and he too was Jewish. Anastasio Petrovich, a pleasure.

'We meet every afternoon at the Café Rex,' he said as he left, hoping in vain that Heinz might buy him a drink. 'Why don't you come by? On Friday, we're holding a big meeting to decide our position on the war.'

'God forbid! There's still a chance it won't happen.'

But there wasn't. While my grandfather and many other incorrigible optimists still clung to the hope of a peaceful solution to a non-existent problem (unless we're to lend credence to Adolf Hitler's demands for *Lebensraum*, living space, no more than a pretext for the *Totensraum* or dead space of war), that night, white carried out what in chess is known as a 'false sacrifice' on the Polish frontier, in the knowledge that he wasn't really risking anything. But to call it false would be too kind: it was plain, dirty cheating, the kind they don't have a name for. He moved one of his opponents' pieces. He'd done this before; sending his pieces to attack his own positions under the guise of the enemy, and now the simulated attack of 31st August on the Gleiwitz radio station, which was famous for its wooden tower, served as a definitive excuse for launching the invasion. The move, one of a series, like the Indian attack on the king, was secretly called Operation Tannenberg. One could well describe it as the perfect anti-chess strategy. A solitary player in no mood for competition, not even with himself, whose only goal is to control the whole board, moves all the pieces under the dozing or incredulous nose of his potential adversaries.

Early on the morning of Friday, the 1st of September, 'shrill sirens announced the prelude to the drama' reported *El Mundo*, referring to the alarm set off by *La Prensa* in its building on Avenida de Mayo in an effort to convey to 'the city and with it the entire country an immediate sense of reality'. *Crítica*, meanwhile, failed to report anything, an injustice that we shall remedy here even if it is under a *nom de plume* (that of the head of the International Section, who made up for the lack of cables with a colourful local story). In the record-breaking issue of *Crítica* ('811,917 copies sold!') under the title 'A Note of Real Drama to the Sound of Sirens', Renzi (grandfather) described the immediate sense of reality conveyed, which it oughtn't be too difficult for us to imagine even after all these years:

Just as the darkness of the night was beginning to give way to the first rays of dawn, sirens shrieked their lament to interrupt the city's sleep. At that intermediate, depressing, unsettling hour when shadow does battle with light, the acute wail of the sirens, a prolonged expression of agony, left the inhabitants of Buenos Aires in no doubt that a tragedy had occurred. After the initial moment of confusion, only one word came to the mind of anyone who heard it: war. But as yet nothing was known. All that could be heard was the undulating screech cutting through the darkness, knocking on every door, and lingering in every window like a howl in the night, or the howl of the world. The city was shaken from its slumber, stomachs clenching at the prospect of this new climate of fear.

Although the events in question are occurring 11,000 kilometres away, the sound of the alarm in the night spread fear just the same; it is no great leap to imagine the terror caused by the sirens of the invaded territories, announcing the arrival of waves of bombers.

People 'in various states of undress' came out en masse to read on large blackboards, not dissimilar to the oversized chess boards, what they already knew; at least those somewhat familiar with the game being played who looked at things rationally rather than emotionally (if one can describe a mutual wish for destruction as rational). Braving a cold more appropriate to the continent where the events were occurring (at 5.55 a.m., it was 5.6 degrees Centigrade), local residents started chatting about the match and speculating on the potential players, who would only be announced on Sunday, when the sirens would ring out again early that morning to announce that 'the final hope for peace has gone up in smoke'.

'Let's see what Chamberlain says.'

'Let's see what Stalin does.'

'Chamberlain's speech was worthy of the Nobel Prize for Literature.'

'Hitler was nominated for the Nobel Peace prize last year. This wouldn't have happened if they'd given it to him.'

'Nor if they'd have given him Danzig.'

'The Germans need *Danzing-raum*.'

'Why don't they come out to Patagonia? They can have as much of it as they like.'

'Shut up, or the Jews will take it instead.'

'Mazel tov!'

'I wonder whether our president has the balls to declare war on that maniac.'

'He'd be the maniac. We need to stay neutral, that way we can sell wheat to everyone.'

'You wouldn't happen to own a farm, would you?'

'It's the Russkies that keep me up at night.'

'I feel the same way about their devotchkas.'

'My, my!'

'But I mean it: the important thing is what the Russians do.'

'The Russians aren't playing.'

'Of course they are. I reckon they're in league with the Poles.'

'But Germany will beat them easily: they have Austria.'

'That's not the same thing.'

'Still, I think our team has a chance.'

'What team?'

'Wait, aren't we talking about the chess tournament?'

'The one they played at Luna Park the other night?'

But the discussion shouldn't have been about the players, who would be joined by others and some of whom would change sides. It should have been about the board: that was the big novelty of the conflict. Although it would later become known as the second, it was in fact the first of them all, at least in the sense that it was being played according to new rules, rules as momentous as the one making the queen the most versatile piece or the one allowing pawns to be queened. And not the invention of a wonderful new weapon; Hitler's V2 of course (the only thing able to defeat Vera Menchik de Stevenson), but more importantly Albert Einstein's atomic one. The war would be the first to feel the brunt of its destructive power, which over time has only increased; he who bombs last, bombs hardest (ha!) Just as the First World War saw the invention of the hypermodern chess school, which introduced new weapons such as the Indian defence (see Rinder vs Karff) and placed ideological conflicts over the nature of the game centre stage, the Second would be the first to impose the ideology-warfare model in which the combatants remained the same while the field of battle; the board, changed. As in the aforementioned poem by Borges, which was blatantly influenced by Omar Khayyam, superpowers lined up behind each country, reducing the players to the status of pieces.

The first to see this, again, was Borges but now in his story 'The Secret Miracle' which is about war but also chess. The ubiquity of the metaphor of chess for war (or war as a game of chess) means that it's always in danger of becoming meaningless, or at best assuming the dubious power of a tautology but when it is as obvious as this it remains powerful, like invoking the etymological meaning of a word when the context calls for it, even if it ends up making us look irredeemably pompous (for instance; the word 'chess' is a bastardization of the Middle English 'chesse', which is a bastardization of the plural of the Old French word 'eschec', which is a bastardization of Medieval Latin 'scaccus', which is a bastardization of the Arabic word 'sah', which is a bastardization of the Persian word 'šāh' [king], which is a bastardization of the Middle Persian word 'šāh', which is a bastardization of the Old Persian word 'xšāyaθiya', which is a bastardization of the Proto-Indian-Iranian word 'kšáyati' [he rules, has power over], which is a bastardization of the Proto-Indo-European 'tek' [to gain power over, gain control over]). So, in 'The Secret Miracle'—a story about the greatest *Wunderwaffe* of them all, literary invention, the only thing that is absolutely bomb-proof, and set in 1939 while the Nazis were entering Czechoslovakia—the author of the unfinished tragedy 'The Enemies' dreams of a long game of chess contested 'not by two individuals but two noble families' which 'had been going one for centuries'. It was the one about to be fought now and for many generations to come between the ideologies of Karl Marx and Adam Smith.

12

SECRETLY PLANNING

Trembling with rage, or rather desire, but an ill-intentioned desire, one that arose out of both general malevolence and the general good; trembling, then, with hatred and unfamiliar emotions, or with confusion at hateful feelings inappropriate in an aspiring rabbi and intellectual; trembling with gritted teeth and a sweaty hand, Heinz Magnus wrote on Sunday, the 3rd of September 1939, the line: 'Let's hope that the criminal gets his head cracked open.'

I may not be a graphologist but I can feel the anger emanating from that sentence, one that tangibly drips with death. These feelings must have been so deeply felt that even today they jump out at me, overpowering the smell of the black notebook in which it was written, an aroma that over time has come to be the smell of my grandfather. He always smelt of paper, did Grandpa Heinz. First that of the books from his library, and then his diaries and letters, which, in a way, are the books he wrote. I can't help but rub the pages between my fingers, like a cat trying to imprint something with its scent.

'*Wollen wir hoffen, dass dieser Verbrecher bald den Hals bricht.*' Magnus thought and wrote, gripping the pen so tight that his fingers turned white, as though bloody wishes can only be expressed with the blood of those who feel and express them.

Perhaps this is why they release a distinctive fragrance for as long as they're legible. Or maybe he didn't see it like that; not so personally, if one might put it that way, because it was the armies of other countries who were supposed to kill the scoundrel (who shared the same name as his father, which might explain why it took him so long to personalize his hatred, at least in writing). Maybe these flimsy, ephemeral words weren't calling for an assassination, maybe as he transferred the thought of them into action, so to speak, he was placing the punishment in the hands of the only Judge whose universal authority he recognized. It may have arisen out of desire but what he eventually wrote was a prayer.

Perhaps made aware by his subconscious of that scandalous depersonalization, he left things as they were and went out, determined not to leave them as they were. Even though it was a Sunday, the cold but not overly damp air of the city was broiling with excitement over a sporting event: the Chess Championship at the Politeama. That was how close the combat taking place on the European board felt, maybe due to the number of immigrants familiar with the previous encounter, the First, including Heinz's parents and even Heinz himself, although he was probably too young to remember.

In the autobiography he was writing at the time, which would come out after his suicide, Stefan Zweig explained why the war in 1914 represented a watershed in European and World history:

My father, my grandfather, what did they see? Each of them lived his life in uniformity. A single life from beginning to end, without ascent, without decline, without disturbance or danger, a life of slight anxieties, hardly noticeable transitions. In even rhythm, leisurely and quietly, the wave of time bore them from the cradle to the grave. They lived in the same country, in the same city, and nearly always in the same house. What took place out in the world only occurred in the newspapers and never knocked at their door. In their time some war happened somewhere but, measured by the dimensions of today, it was only a little war. It took place far beyond the border, one did not hear the cannon, and after six months it died down, forgotten, a dry page of history, and the old accustomed life began anew. But in our lives there was no repetition; nothing of the past survived, nothing came back. It was reserved for us to participate to the full in that which history formerly distributed, sparingly and from time to time, to a single country, to a single century. At most, one generation had gone through a revolution, another experienced a putsch, the third a war, the fourth a famine, the fifth national bankruptcy; and many blessed countries, blessed generations, bore none of these. But we, who are 60 today and who, de jure, still have a space of time before us, what have we not seen, not suffered, not lived through?

To put it in chess terms to which perhaps even Zweig himself might have subscribed, it was as though the inhabitants of those lands had gone from living like kings, or bishops at least, to being pawns who aren't allowed to go back over their steps. But the real pawns would be those of the coming generations who never even experienced 'The World of Yesterday', as Zweig calls it, in the most absolute sense of the term. These pieces, which never even get to experience the first file on the board, feel a particular nostalgia for their isolated past—not so much their origins as the unreachable progenitor of all that would come later.

Perhaps in the subconscious knowledge that this new European war was a kind of personal revenge for the previous one, and that it was apparently also taking place in a theatre in Buenos Aires, Magnus headed back to the centre, instinctively repeating the move he'd planned to make the previous Thursday. On this occasion, however, it was inspired more by hatred than romance. Maybe he too saw it as revenge. The vitality he had lost after the failed date with the chess player at *La Bête Humane*; there was a good reason he had interpreted it in metaphorical terms in his diary, going on about sadness and the meaning of life, had returned. His revived euphoria now took him back to the same place from which he'd returned so depressed, as though to show that both swings in mood were part of the same cycle. This would only be properly understood by later generations but he was a bête who had been born with his blood 'poisoned' by a bipolar condition.

The idea of a rematch, a continuation that allows one to rectify what happened and undo it, *aufhebearlo*, as my grandfather would say in the Belgrano Deutsch that he was busy inventing along with his fellow *jecke* immigrants in Buenos Aires, compelled him. Because a match is made up of many different moves and a tournament of many different matches from which scores and rankings are derived, nothing is ever really definitive and nothing ever ends. In this case, Magnus' subconscious desire for a rematch ended up taking shape when he passed by the Café Rex and remembered that the guy from the cinema was meeting with his pacifist friends. On Friday, he'd been too melancholy to go to one of these meetings; he didn't expect anything good to come out of them, and was even a little concerned that they might be anarchists or communists, two creeds for which he had no sympathy whatsoever even if the current situation now saw them on the same side. But now he realized that accepting the Russian's invitation was the best way to heal the wound that had been festering since the German had stood him up, as though he had actually arranged to go to the movies with him, not her. In fact, meeting this man to change the world and not the woman who would, at the most, change his life had a much grander, more expansive feel.

The setting for the meeting was certainly appropriate. It might be germane to note here, taking advantage of the fact that it would take Magnus at least an hour to get there, that it was at the tables of the Café Rex at 800 Calle Corrientes that the collective translation of *Ferdydurke* by Witold Gombrowicz, a Polish writer who'd come to Buenos Aires by chance at the same time as the *Piriápolis*,[6] into Spanish took place. The author himself would refer to this coincidence in very chess-like terms: 'It was as though a giant hand had taken me by the collar to remove me from Poland and dropped me in a lost land in the middle of the ocean, lost but European . . . just a month before the war.'

Regarding the Café Rex, Gombrowicz remembers the following in his oft-celebrated diary:

> *Late in 1943 I caught a cold that gave me a slight fever that I couldn't shake off. At the time, I used to play chess at the Café Rex on Calle Corrientes and Frydman, the director of the games room, a good and noble friend*—also the third board on the Polish team playing (and losing) tonight against the Chilean Letelier at the Politeama, who

---

6 But not on the *Piriápolis*, as some of the more sensational historical accounts would have it (and as we would love to repeat here were it not for the little realist gremlin lurking inside of us.).

> would also stay in Buenos Aires and open a chess salon
> right here, above the Café Rex—*was alarmed by my state*
> *of health and gave me some money to go to the mountains*
> *in Córdoba, which I took very kindly. But when I got to*
> *Córdoba my fever remained until finally, the thermometer*
> *Frydman had given me broke, I bought a new one and . . .*
> *the fever was gone. So I owe my stay of a few months at*
> *La Falda to the fact that Frydman's thermometer exagger-*
> *ated one's temperature by a few decimal points.*

So, my grandfather went to a cafe with all that (future) history. There, he met not Witold Gombrowicz (the stellar appearances of Jorge Luis Borges in the barber shop at Harrods and Macedonio Fernández at the Politeama have used up almost all the budget assigned to *litameos*, or literary cameos[7]) but the man he was looking for, whom we have borrowed from the work of Roberto Arlt.

'Either I've got the day wrong, or these people live here,' Magnus thought when he saw him having a heated but secretive discussion with a group at the back of the cafe around a pair of tables strewn with glasses and bottles. The Russian recognized him and invited him to sit in his seat while he got up to fetch another. Magnus appreciated the gesture and the fact that the conversation didn't come to a halt when he arrived. It was a real collective, he thought, although he was sorry that it was contaminated with atheism (it was the fact that they didn't have a great leader in the sky that made it the perfect collective, Grandpa!) He ended up feeling at ease when a boy no more than 20 years old, started

---

7 And there's one more special guest still to come.

speaking to tie the present situation to one Heinz had already noted in his diary a year before:

Today barely anyone remembers the incredible tension we felt when we were 100 per cent sure that war was coming (reads the entry for 30th October 1938). *We couldn't, or didn't want to, believe that the democracies would sacrifice a democracy to the dictatorship*: Czechoslovakia [Bohemia-Moravia]. *Chamberlain has done Hitler a wonderful service* [at the Munich Summit] *and peace, a horrible peace, reigns over the earth. Apart from the fact that everyone is preparing for war, that Germany has become the leading world power, that almost the entire Czechoslovak Republic has become German, that it won't be long before even the oldest colonies become German too, apart from all that, the worst part is that we, the Jews, are affected in every country in the world as we'll never have a place where we can build a life for ourselves. It won't take 10 years for fascism and nationalism, hand in hand with anti-Semitism, to flood the world and then there'll be nothing left for the Jews. Chamberlain's decision has sealed our fate. Or shall we be assigned somewhere where we might finally develop? Because this constant struggle for survival can only end up ruining a people.*

The speaker didn't just refer to Chamberlain, he also mentioned 'the persecuted' of whom the Jewish people were only tacitly included among other minorities. Of course, the anarchists took pride of place. The conversation then turned to Russia's position, which had become especially problematic for them since the pact with Hitler, and also for Magnus who had never approved of

Stalin but still hoped that he'd stand in the other demon's way. The general position of the table coincided with this desire and even speculated that it might become a reality, but such optimism would be dashed just a few weeks later:

> *The war continues*—reads the 23rd September edition of the *Private Diary*—*Before it began, we were indignant at the Nazi–Russian non-aggression pact but we thought that it could only harm Germany. Then the criminal attacked Poland and while he was doing that, Russia attacked Poland too. A shiver ran through us. Was Russia trying to help Germany? Now we see: they invaded to damage Germany. They block his path to the borders with Hungary and Romania so that the murderer is prevented from getting to his true objective. He wanted to 'cross to the East'. He has been stopped from doing that. I am firmly convinced that the democracies will triumph although there will be great losses and much sacrifice. Only God knows what will come after this war, which will surely be long.*

Surprised that he agreed with these people's vision of the world (part of it anyway), the past and their hopes for the future (part of them anyway), finally feeling part (partly) of a collective that wasn't his and encouraged (in no little part) by the Quilmes beer with which his green glass (partly frosted) was being consistently refilled, Magnus finally took advantage of a brief lull (someone got up to go to the bathroom and someone ordered more beer as though they had to ensure that the amount of liquid contained in bottles, glasses and bladders remained constant) to answer someone who only a few hours earlier had depersonalized the struggle to the point of minimizing it, i.e. himself.

'Something must be done,' he said, perhaps to himself, lingering on the vowel sounds as he'd noticed plenty doing at the table. 'Something real.'

The exhortation exploded like a bomb. You wouldn't have got such an energetic response if you'd suggested a theory of everything at a congress of quantum mechanics.

'An attack, I agree,' said someone with a moustache.

'No, not quite that real,' Magnus said, frightened. Before anything else he was a pacifist (although the question at the time wasn't what one was *before anything else* but what one is willing to do *after everything has happened*.) 'I was thinking of something more symbolic, a message.'

With their minds suddenly occupied with an explosive device, specifically the one that the anarchist Simón Radowitzky had thrown at Captain Falcón in 1909, it was hard to conceive of a symbolic attack—in the style of Marcel Duchamp's urinal; the artist was a keen chess player and he too was eventually moved by a giant hand (the one that moves men across the board) to Buenos Aires.[8]

---

8 *As unlikely as it sounds*—says Julio Cortázar in *Around the Day in Eighty Worlds*—*this trip is an excellent example of the vagaries of chance that some of us literary irregulars continue to explore. For my part, I am sure that fate had a hand, as is proven by the first page of* Impressions d'Afrique: *'15 March, 19. . . , intending to embark on a long journey through the curious regions of South America, I set sail from Marseilles on board the Lyncée, a fast packet boat of sizeable tonnage on the Buenos Aires line.' Duchamp surely figured among the passengers who would fill Raymond Roussel's incomparable book with the poetry of the exceptional. He must have travelled incognito because he's never mentioned, but I am certain he played chess with Roussel . . .*

Magnus' second exhortation to do something 'more symbolic' appeared to exceed the revolutionaries' imaginative capabilities until the person who'd just been interacting with a urinal spoke up:

'Che, who's winning the chess tournament?'

'Argentina man, who else?' answered the most native man at the table. And yet, under the Nuremberg laws he would have been forbidden from marrying a truly indigenous person. 'Then come Poland and Germany.'

'Poland and Germany no less!'

Cortázar adds that it's logical for 'serious critics', as he calls them, to assert that none of this is possible (but following our inverted move of placing Mirko Czentovich in 'Argentina', we know otherwise, don't we?) but the truth is that the critic Graciela Speranza, the author of the very serious *Duchamp in Argentina*, says:

> The mention of Buenos Aires in Roussel's book is no mean encourage-ment for our exploration of 1918. The 'madness of the unexpected' that Duchamp saw in the theatrical adaptation of Impressions d'Afrique *in Paris in 1911 made Roussel his leading artistic light. 'Roussel is the main person responsible for my glass,' he would say in 1946. [. . .] Cortázar's speculation has a certain logic to it; where Roussel had led the way with the terrifying aftermath of the wreck of a ship headed for Buenos Aires, why not take the master's fiction at his word and head for Buenos Aires?*

The 'glass' Duchamp alludes to, which is actually called 'To be looked at (from the other side of the glass) with one eye, close up, for almost an hour', is the only artwork that he produced in the nine months that he spent in Buenos Aires. He spent most of his time playing chess. His obsession with the game, which he of course saw as an art, not in the sense that everything was, even a urinal, but the opposite one that held that a urinal was a urinal and a pipe was a pipe, i.e. that of those who believed that his output, including his 'glass' wasn't art, however you wanted to look at it. His obsession with the art of the board grew so compelling that, according to Juan Sebastián Morgado in *Lights and Shadows of Argentine Chess*, 'his lover Yvonne Chastel got tired of him and left for Paris alone. Before leaving the department on Calle Alsina, she glued the pieces to the board . . .'

'That's it!' Magnus exclaimed with the excitement of someone who recognizes the artistic power of an object. 'The chess tournament is the perfect place to send a message to the whole world.'

'I agree, we need to set off a bomb,' the advocate of violence, a skinny 40-something with a gaunt face, and liver too, probably, piped up again. Although he claimed theoretically to be ready for anything involving force, he looked as though it was all he could do to lift his glass and cigarettes.

'You want to set off a bomb at the Politeama Theatre?' Magnus exclaimed incredulously.

'I don't know how big it is. Maybe one won't be enough, we might have to plant two or three,' said the man without a hint of irony.

'The other option would be to kidnap the German team,' suggested the Argentine first class (the only one among them who had actually been to school in Argentina).

'Good idea, but the two projects don't have to be mutually exclusive,' the gaunt man insisted. While the others plunged head-long into an argument about which or both options would be the best course of action or whether there was a third even better one (take the theatre hostage, take the embassy hostage, overthrow the government, another Quilmes please!), Petrovich, who was sitting next to Heinz, tried to explain to him that good intentions didn't get you anywhere in this world, as was evidenced by the case of Poland which was now suffering the aggression of its neighbour because they hadn't made the first move ('I thought they did attack first,' said a misguided *Crítica* reader nearby). Magnus understood this position, he even felt it, why else had he written a few hours earlier that he wanted not to defeat the criminal, not to make him lay down his arms and put him on trial, but to crack his head open, to crush it until he heard the crunch of bone and saw the blood begin to flow (rip-roaring regicide)? But Hitler was one thing and a few chess players who had little or nothing to do with him, not to mention the audience, was something else. But it was the fact that they had nothing to do with the real objective of the attack that made it symbolic, Petrovich argued, to which Magnus replied that that was all very well but the bloodshed wouldn't be. By that logic, he went on, everything is symbolic. Including the deportation and murder of thousands of Jews . . . and anarchists, he finished just to make sure that his point struck home.

'You're taking things to an extreme,' said Petrovich.

'No more than you,' Magnus replied.

They agreed to bring their sidebar to an end and join the rest of the group, which at the time was discussing their chances of being able to sink any German ships sailing near the Argentinian coast (the Graf Spee would be arriving shortly and would indeed be sunk, not that this proto-terrorist cell had anything to do with it). Petrovich waited for a gap in the conversation to remind the group that their operational capacities were limited (just organizing these meetings was a lot of work; in fact, their existence owed more to the fact that they all happened to go to the Café Rex to drink beer every afternoon). Instead, to Magnus' surprise and pleasure, he suggested taking advantage of the symbolic value not just of the tournament but also the game itself with a simple but effective attack.

'A flash bomb,' said the gaunt man.

'All bark and no bite,' said someone a little more erudite.

'Let's make sure Argentina wins,' said the Argentinian.

'Or Poland at least,' countered Petrovich.

'But that would be cheating!' said the one who had suggested raiding the theatre one night and killing the hostages one by one until all their comrades were released from their different prisons across the world.

'The important thing is for Germany not to win,' said Magnus through gritted teeth. 'The Germans have never won an Olympiad and it would be a catastrophe were they to do so now.' Petrovich raised his glass and the others followed suit.

'They shall not win!' he exclaimed with the ingenuity of someone who doesn't know that everything has already been written.

'They shall not win!' chorused the rest with the confidence of those who know that the pen that writes our fate can also be used to strike things out.

13

A PEACEFUL DUEL

Sonja Graf opened *Murphy* by Samuel Beckett, the last book she'd bought before setting sail, and put it on the table (if Buenos Aires were a chessboard and its inhabitants were pieces, then the squares would be provided by cafe tables). She opened it to page 243 and suggested reproducing the match between Murphy and Endon described there. Mirko Czentovic heard the former as Paul Morphy, the American player who only failed to beat all comers because some refused to come (leading him to take his leave of chess, then his sanity and, ultimately, his life), and instinctively took his place because he didn't like losing, not even when the match had been played by someone else, in the past, and there was nothing to be gained.

By the fifth move, however, Czentovic had realized that there was something odd, or even morbid about this game. Something anti-chess. He continued because Graf didn't seem to have noticed, or had already noticed and was now looking beyond it, at something that he hadn't yet perceived. As they went on, the match grew more absurd: the pieces came and went for no good reason, timid attacks without consequence. For some moves, the players even checked, like in poker. Although none of the moves were illegal, the fact that they didn't damage the opponent made them more suspicious still, as though they were using legitimate weapons to commit the worst of crimes: not trying to win. Czentovic knew it would end in a draw but only because he'd seen the annotation at the end of the game on the next page. The way they were playing, it could easily go on for ever. So it wouldn't come as a surprise, or affront, when, following a scandalous series of unfinished sallies by white whose pieces were spread across the board while black's had barely shifted from their starting position (none of the black pieces had crossed to the other side of the board, as though an un-fordable river ran across the middle), Czentovic suddenly realized that he was the one who was supposed to give up.

'But we haven't taken a single piece!' he exclaimed with an absolutely humourless smile. Graf maintained an enigmatic silence and Czentovic asked whether it was like the backward game they'd played when they met. Or was it one of those magical games of chess with special rules and strange pieces? Sonja gave him a quizzical look. Without seeing the trap that had been laid (on the board, he saw them all, but in real life Czentovic was endearingly naive, which is why Sonja had taking a liking to him and was spending so much time with him, not to mention the fact that she, too, was boyish by nature) or that Beckett's game wasn't serious, not even under the dubiously serious terms of so-called fairy chess, Czentovic spent some time talking about his favourite alternative pieces: the Grasshopper (which can only move if it has a piece to jump over), the Reversible Pawn (which can go backward) and the Imitator (which does just that, imitating a piece when it moves but that can't take or be taken). He also mentioned oval, duplicate and three-dimensional boards and the awkward versions where white tries to get mated or both colours working to mate just one of them, like a coup d'etat with help from inside the government (the board, in fact, is like city walled in behind four towers inside which a war of succession fought between two kings rages unendingly). But although Czentovic appreciated the novelty of these flights of fancy, he didn't think they had much real value other than having taught him that orthodox chess was just another variation. It even had its own fantastical pieces like the knight, not to mention strange moves like castling on the queen's side and the miracle of queening.

'Those moves are like irregular verbs—they teach us that the language we use could easily have other rules,' Czentovic concluded to Sonja's surprise, and even our own: the way Zweig describes him he sounds barely literate (never underestimate a piece's potential!)

Sonja, who thought she was the only one who appreciated these facets of a game she'd learnt as though it really were a language (but not to the point of feeling, like Czentovic, that anyone who didn't play, or who played badly, was indeed illiterate). She closed her mouth, that had gaped open in amazement, and wondered whether the idea of chess as a random variation among a thousand other possibilities was the reason that the kid refused to study any other forms of language. Over the past few days, she'd realized that chess was his entire life: she hadn't managed to get him interested in anything beyond the board or the Politeama (although she certainly didn't want to become the focus of that interest herself; for that she already had Yanofsky and, maybe, maybe, the young man from the barber shop). The odd thing about Czentovic was that for him chess seemed to offer a religious-style basis for everything else. Maybe that was why he cared so much about his clothes; he was trying to cover up the starkness of his obsessions. But it was a starkness that included a lack of pockets, which explained why he never had any money on him. Sonja saw every move as a verse and every game as a more or less complete poem, she saw beauty in its shifts and real problems in its dilemmas but she had never become obsessed, not even now that she played every day. In contrast to tobacco, and alcohol to a minor extent (not to mention sweets), the idea of indulging until it became an addiction was somewhat upsetting. She didn't see why it should necessarily be true that something one enjoys should lead to a compulsion, unless there were solid chemical reasons, but this obsession seemed widespread in the world of chess. Just as scientists are mad, cooks fat and poets consumptive, the chess player is always obsessed with the game. Or at least that was true of chess players in the popular imagination.

Literary depictions didn't help matters; there was Mirko Czentovic of course, but also Tony, whom Graf had met in Berlin a few years ago. Tony was a character from *The Gambit*, the novel the father of Luzhin, the chess player featured in the novel *The Defence* by Vladimir Nabokov, could never quite finish. In said novel (Luzhin's father's and part of Nabokov's), set in a cafe in Berlin, a young chess prodigy must die so as not to become the heartbroken creature the writer's son had been. But because the writer dies before finishing it (or maybe before beginning it, given that one of his ideas was to start with the ending), the character grew up and became the surly man that his father (or stepfather in the novel within the novel) so feared.

Sonja Graf, who knew none of that (Tony only had a vague idea of it, the way someone who is solely interested in the match they're playing only has a vague idea of the origins of the game), had met the young man with the heavy-lidded eyes and extremely pale skin (the curls he'd been described as having in *The Gambit* were long gone) once his period as a child prodigy was long behind him. Now he earned a living teaching or playing for money in cafes. You would expect that a brilliant man condemned to such a lowly lifestyle would hate the game, or at least see it as no more than a means to an end but failure didn't seem to have had any effect on Tony's passion for chess. Quite to the contrary, he continued to be obsessed with the 64 squares just as much as when he'd toured the cities of Europe with his stepfather playing simultaneous games. It was as though this major part of his childhood had grown up with him, preventing him from finding anything else to do as an adult. This single-minded man, like a character created with a single idea, was the first perfectly stereotypical chess player Graf had met.

Sonja was fascinated by Tony, maybe because he embodied all the passion for the game that she had never been able to summon. To her relative relief, she soon understood that the mania had nothing in common with what one associates with enthusiasm or even determination. If Tony was a prisoner of his passion, as they say, it was in the least metaphorical sense of the term. He had told her that deep down he wasn't moving the pieces but that an invisible force emanating from the pieces themselve—the force they had over each other on the board—compelled him to make such and such a move. The Borgesian question about what god lay behind the first God in the line of succession that ended with the player moving the pieces now had a definitive if wholly unexpected answer: the chain began at the beginning, with the board itself.

'Everything all right?' asked Czentovic, jolting her out of her reverie.

'Everything all thought-out!'

Only when Sonja told him that the author of the book, which she was quick to clarify was not a collection of chess problems, orthodox or otherwise, but just a simple novel, or not that simple but still a novel; only when she told Czentovic that Beckett knew a lot about chess, as she'd found out herself when she'd played him in a Parisian cafe that Marcel Duchamp also frequented, although the fantasy that they'd played each other was apparently as baseless as the idea that Hitler and Lenin had played each other, the suggestion arising from a painting from the beginning of the century (Hitler did, however, meet Franz Kafka, as Ricardo Piglia documented in his novel *Artificial Respiration*); only after Graf had presented the chess-playing credentials of the Irish writer did Czentovic start to respect him and try to look for meaning in the absurd game they'd reproduced on the board. First, he started drawing lines on a napkin tracing out the different moves they'd played to see if they formed some kind of image, maybe the letters of one of the languages he'd never learnt; or so Stefan Zweig says—we're starting to doubt the accuracy of his biography (the pieces are moving the player). After pushing these scribbles to one side—you could see whatever you liked in them if you looked hard enough—the not-so-illiterate (given that he was at least well versed in the language of chess) boy asked Graf to read out Beckett's commentary on the match between Murphy and Endon. Neither did this new approach lead anywhere, not even the comic phrases, including '*An ingenious and beautiful debut, sometimes called the Pipe-opener,*' or '*High praise is due to White for the pertinacity with which he struggles to lose a piece,*' left much room for serious interpretation. Seeing Czentovic analysing a literary problem as though it were a chess puzzle did at least lead Sonja somewhere, namely, to the conclusion that although she wasn't obsessed with the game herself, she was certainly fascinated by those who did suffer from the condition, perhaps to a more dangerous degree than the chess players themselves.

'I give up,' said Czentovic, giving up. 'The man who made up that game was either a joker or a madman.'

'According to Lasker, there's nothing more difficult in chess than a comic move.'

'But this isn't chess!'

'So what is chess, then?'

Czentovic frowned. The question was so obvious that he couldn't think of an answer. All the different definitions that occurred to him (it's a game, a science, an art, etc.) twisted themselves into questions (What is a game? What is a science? etc.) and his brain foundered in stalemate.

'I know what it is, but if you ask me I feel that I don't,' he said unwittingly (or not) citing Saint Augustine's definition of time.

'I'll tell you: chess is an emotion born of anxious expectancy suddenly dwindling into nothing,' Graf said, wittingly citing Immanuel Kant's famous definition of laughter.

Before her companion was able to take this in, not that he'd even understand that it was a joke, Sonja gave him a solution to the conundrum. The match in *Murphy* was a pacifist manifesto, which is why the players moved the pieces at random, or for purely aesthetic reasons without taking pieces, not even when they were at a clear advantage. Deep down they didn't want to hurt each other, only to act freely within the agreed-upon rules in the hope that they might one day be in a position to create new ones (not to hurt each other might actually be considered the first).

Beckett had chosen the quintessential metaphor for war to create a playful metaphor for peace before war had even been declared.

'Wouldn't it be wonderful if Germany and Poland agreed to play that game?' Graf said, finally getting the conversation where she wanted it.

'The same one? If it were real, maybe,' Czentovic said grumpily; like all characters, he mistrusted fiction (the way waiters don't eat at the restaurant where they work, and doctors choose a different hospital to their own to have their operations).

'It's real now, we just played it. We'd have to play it again to return it to its own reality, or it'll stay in this one for ever.'

14

A GRAND CONSPIRACY

The chess historian Franklin Knowles Young reconstructed the Battle of Waterloo 'as historically and technically illustrated on a chessboard'. As he says in the appendix to the book *Chess Strategetics Illustrated* (1900), it involved a Ruy López opening in which black, (the French), unusually, moved first:

1. P - K4.

(11 A.M.) Prince Jerome, younger brother of the Emperor, opens the battle of Waterloo by attacking the Park of Hougoumont.

1. P - K 4.

Ponsonby's English dragoons covering La Haye Sainte.

2. Kt - KB 3.

Milhaud's cuirassiers taking position in support of the coming assault against the English centre.

2. Q Kt - B 3.

Bylandt's Dutch and Belgians advancing in support of La Haye Sainte.

3. K B - Kt 5.

French light cavalry moving against the English left wing.

3. P - Q K 3

(12.30 P.M.) Advance guard of the German Fourth Army Corps occupying St. Lambert.

4. B - R 4.

Gen. D'Homond taking post at Pajeau on the lookout for the expected French right wing under Marshal Grouchy.

4 Kt - K B 3.

English regular troops moving to the support of Hougoumont.

5. P - Q B 3.

Jaquinoi's lancers advancing to the attack of La Haye Sainte.

5. P - QKt4.

Billow's vanguard driving back French light cavalry.

6. B - B 2.

The Sixth French Corps d'Armée under Count Lobau masses about Planchenoit to cover the French rear and right wing against Bülow.

6. KB - B4.

Yandeleur's cavalry opening up communication with Bülow, and covering English left wing.

7. Castles.

Napoleon and the Imperial Guard taking position on the heights of La Belle Alliance.

7. Castles.

The Duke of Wellington and his reserves taking position at Mont St. Jean.

8. P - Q4.

(1 P.M.) Marshal Ney leads D'Erlon's corps to the attack of the English left and centre.

8. P X P.

Overthrow of Durutte's division by Ponsonby's dragoons.

9. P X P.

Ponsonby's dragoons destroyed bj Jaquinot's lancers. D'Erlon carries Souhain by the bayonet.

9. B - K2.

Vandeleur's cavalry falling back on Mont St. Jean before D'Erlon.

Here, the chessologist interrupts his account to note: 'This movement in defence of the right wing seems forced: for if 9. B - Kt 3, P - K 5 : 10. Kt - K sq. B X R P (ck.; 11. K x B, Kr - Kr 5 (ck); 12. K - Kt sq. Q - K P 5: and Black wins.'

It seems that he did all that work transcribing the game just so he could introduce this note: black had made an unforced error that might have been avoided, for example by the move that Young genially proposes, which would have led to a rapid victory. The only possible reason to suggest a hypothetical alternative to a very real battle is a desire to win the war in Napoleon's shoes.

'And who is it that likes to put himself in Napoleon's shoes?' exclaimed Adolfo Magnus pointedly, glaring at his son Heinz.

'. . .'

'Who is it that believes they can win a war with toy weapons?' he went on loudly.

'. . .'

Adolfo Magnus had shifted from passive defence to a more forthright attack at his son Heinz's suggestion that he'd noticed (and noted down) that his father's mind had begun to wander since they'd been forced out of Germany.

For some time, I have noticed that my father is getting older (he says in April 1938). *His hearing has grown noticeably worse, he forgets things, repeats himself, is irritable and more than anything is very critical of Ludwig* [Heinz's sister Astarte's husband].

The argument had begun after Heinz had brought up the idea of his mother baking cakes again. This was rejected outright by his father and sister, who had told him that the only one who ought to be earning more money was him, not his elderly mother (she wasn't particularly elderly; only 56, although she would go on to die in a few years' time). Heinz had raised the issue again after outlining a vague plan to interrupt the chess tournament (or the course of the war, depending on how you looked at it), which had met with the family's enthusiastic approval. Only when dinner was over did he realize that they weren't so much pleased at his plan as they were enjoying the cannelloni (vegetable of course, in keeping with the kosher diet) with white sauce that he'd brought home to celebrate the modest raise of 5 pesos a month he'd received in September.

He left the table without finishing his dessert (one of his mother's famous cakes, upside-down with caramelized apples) and locked himself in his room. They were lodgers in a traditional long, narrow house in the Colegiales neighbourhood with a chess-board patio (a feature Heinz would only notice that week), a shared well and two bathrooms at the back for all residents. Although this might sound like modest accommodation given there were 11 people in all, it was better than that enjoyed by the Polish team. See the already cited answer of the team captain Savielly Tartakower when asked who would win the tournament:

> *Probably the Argentinian team because their accommoda-tion will almost certainly be excellent. We Poles have to share a bathroom between five of us. Whoever uses it last will inevitably arrive late for their match. This morning, I washed up before seven, in the dark, in consideration of my teammates, who also need to wash. It's a good thing I remembered where my nose was. Our only consolation is the thought that the other teams must be suffering in sim-ilar conditions.*

The interview in *Noticias Gráficas* also includes other memorable passages that, now that the game is truly afoot, as they say, there seems no good reason not to repeat here:

> *'This tournament is notable particularly for the nation that is missing: the United States of America, who have won it on four occasions.'*
>
> *'Do you believe that they would have won it a fifth time?'*
>
> *'I firmly believe that they wouldn't have. They won it the first time because nobody was expecting it. The second*

because everyone was afraid of them. The third because no one expected them to win it three times in a row and the fourth because we all contributed to their win—we were resigned to it. But why would they have won a fifth time? There's nothing to suggest they would.'

'Let's discuss the international political situation.'

'My opinions on that subject aren't important at all. They are exact, precise, logical and reasonable. Right now, the world has grown somewhat hysterical and prefers to applaud nonsense. Later, perhaps, a time will come when more rational opinions are back in fashion. Then I shall be an overwhelming success as a thinker and countries will surely contract my services as a statesman. Meanwhile, you'll forgive me if I don't share the system I have devised to fix the international situation.'

'No we shan't sir. Reasonable opinions still find a hearing in Argentina.'

'Well then, certainly, if that's truly the case then I shall give away my recipe for free. When two countries wish to quarrel, they should submit to the result of a game of chess. The losing chess player shall have his head cut off. In that simple manner, wars, rather than subjecting millions to misery, plague and destruction, shall be resolved by a single death. The lowest price imaginable.'

But Heinz Magnus dreamt of something cheaper still. Alone and in the dark, like a chess player mentally preparing for his next match, he was putting the finishing touches to a master plan that had been brewing over the past few days. It was designed to

ensure that Germany, and if possible Argentina, would be prevented from winning. Ideally, the trophy would go to Tartakower's
team so that the Poles would be able to take it back to Europe as
a symbol of reason and resistance.

The plan to manipulate the matches was inspired by the Poe
text he'd cited to Czentovic, Graf and the other chess player
whose name now escaped him and eventually would the world
the other night. Like Maelzel's Turk, which, much to Poe's disgust,
was probably the most successful automaton in history, the idea
was to smuggle players under the tables to help the weaker teams
beat Germany or at least to deprive them of points that would
then give a boost to the Poles, perhaps subliminally but certainly
under the table.

At first he considered fitting a table with magnets to mirror
the pieces' moves on the underside so that the hidden player could
follow the match from their hiding place. But it would be too risky
to use the same method to pass their responses back topside.
Looking for a solution to this basic problem, Magnus realized that
it could be done without touching the board at all. They could
simply work out a kind of Morse code that allowed them to communicate using the feet of the player above and the hands of the
player below. One foot for the columns, the other for the rows
and both, previously, for the piece. Hands and feet would be in
constant contact and messages would be tapped out softly.
Magnets might still be useful, he realized, because they would
allow the ringer to follow their opponent's moves and ensure that
his ally was doing the right thing, thus reducing the need for code.

But the plan still had some weaknesses. Primarily, it required
too many people. This could be resolved through close study of

the fixture list and identification of where intervention would be necessary. It also seemed unlikely that they'd be able to find enough players better than their competitors who also matched the physical specifications; they needed to be small and flexible. Finally, there was the issue of how to get them under the tables, which needed to be prepared beforehand unbeknownst to the tournament organizers in order to prevent discovery. The last thing he wanted was for the bullet to go off when still in the chamber, especially from a gun loaded by a Jew.

The image of a Jew playing the devil reminded him of a cartoon that showed a heavily bearded God in a white tunic talking to a priest in a classic black cassock from which a devil's tail pokes out the back. He couldn't remember where he'd seen the blasphemous drawing or what it was trying to say but he didn't care: the idea it gave him justified having remembered it. He could smuggle the hidden player into the room under a priest's cassock. The priest could say he was blessing the tables and thus get close enough for the little devil he was hiding to take his position without anyone noticing. In fact (Magnus thought in the same breath, as though inspiration were a pool you had to dive into and stay immersed in for as long as you could), the pregnant priest could even walk between the tables, ferrying a single Turk from board to board, like a player playing simultaneous games.

Now I have to find the right priest, Magnus said to himself, trying to contain his euphoria with the consideration of another obstacle (or trying to ride his euphoria over said obstacle). It occurred to him that the minister ought to be German so as not to arouse the suspicion of the Germans and also so he could distract them in their own language. Of course, it had to be a German who opposed the regime, militantly if possible. A priest who would play in the name of freedom, like the chess player who'd stood him up at the cinema. All of which meant that this was a good excuse to see her, as he was reasoning (with more than his head) when his sister came into the room and turned on the light.

'He's old, pay him no mind,' she said, getting straight to the point.

'He doesn't know how much easier it would have been for me to leave Germany on my own,' Heinz lied. He'd have rather gone voluntarily to a death camp before leaving his parents to such a fate.

'He knows, we all know,' Astarte said encouragingly.

'But when it comes to helping out, your rings fall off,' he said, trying out one of the Spanish phrases he was so enjoying learning to use.

Then he explained to his sister that as a son *one has a duty to their parents, but they also exist in a certain social layer. That brings with it certain unseen commitments that are harder, more urgent and guilt-ridden than one may realize. Because parents are an indivisible part of that social layer and with it their 'life and world-view'*, Heinz went on. The onus was on him: he had to *earn money, act like a social animal and form a part of certain social groups.*

'*Of course one can break with that "society" even if it isn't easy (because of the parents) but not when one is alone. You have to do it with someone else, and it's not time yet.*'

'I hope that it'll be a long time before that, if it means you breaking with everyone,' his sister said, smiling with mischief but also a little fear.

'Of course, so you don't have to find a job!'

'I didn't mean that, Adonis!'

'I don't mind having to do it, the problem is that I'm breaking my back and even so just barely covering our expenses.'

'You can't expect much more in our situation. Maybe deep down the person losing his rings is my brother the intellectual, with his libertine dreams.'

Heinz rejected the image and so only made it stronger. *It is surely a shame that I don't earn enough money to be a little more carefree. I am happy with my studies* [of languages] *and believe that I'm making steady progress but I often feel as though I'm not learning anything new. It would be nice to have enough spare time to read books as well. But given that I'm planning to live for a good few years yet, these wishes will surely come to pass.*

'*Sometimes I think that only the tension between desire and reality makes life tolerable and that if it were ever removed I'd slip into depression very easily,*' Heinz added. '*Because when it comes to the meaning of life, I haven't advanced an iota.*'

Astarte's face crinkled into a sceptical frown and she wondered aloud whether the tension between desire and reality that her brother so cherished wasn't in fact the main cause of his depression, or at least what set it off. Heinz explained that he meant the need to have dreams even when life was difficult so as to preserve hope for the future.

'*My fantasy is to be lying on a bed or in a meadow somewhere. I close my eyes. Invisible rays flow inside me. The content of these rays isn't well defined but the longer they glow within me, the more I apprehend their message. I open my eyes and get up. I am a new man. I know the meaning of the world. Nothing can happen to me. Is that what perfection feels like?'*

Astarte shook her head, rejecting the idea that such a mystical union could be possible or even desirable. She repeated her belief that the tension between the desire to find the meaning of life and reality of not getting an answer must be quite pernicious to the soul. Especially for a soul like Heinz's, which was especially sensitive. She suggested making peace with the urge to get what he wanted; a little more money and a woman to share it with. They would come sooner or later.

'Sometimes I think that your metaphysical desires are just a cover for your earthly ones,' she said eventually but immediately regretted her cruelty.

'Perhaps,' said Heinz who tended to contradict his sister by telling her that she was right before sending some of that self-righteousness back her way with a double helping of cruelty. 'But that doesn't mean that one's pecuniary ambitions, for example marrying a man who will surely make you rich with his orthopaedics, are any more spiritual.'

Either because she was confident that his prediction would come true (and time would show that it would, the only problem being that the inheritance would go to the children of Ludwig's second wife, a plague on their finances) or at least because she didn't want to jinx it, Astarte chose to let the jibe pass (gambit repulsed) and invited him to the theatre. Her husband was away on business.

'What if we go to the chess tournament?'

'Another day, right now you need to clear your mind.'

15

GOOD INTENTIONS AND MISUNDERSTANDINGS

Yanofksy's next move was to invite Sonja Graf to dinner at his flat under the pretext of introducing her to his friend Ezequiel Martínez Estrada (our surprise guest!) The writer from Santa Fe, who recently won an award for his book *Radiografía de la Pampa* (X-ray of the Pampas) was a huge chess fan. The aforementioned 'X-ray' was more of a reference to the *Röntgenangriff* attack, named for the German doctor who discovered X-rays, than X-rays themselves. Yanofksy invited him because of this and because he was his most intellectual friend. This was an area where he found Sonja particularly challenging, so he planned to use his erudite friend as bait for his prey, who would presumably stick around once the writer had withdrawn.

The dinner went very well. They spoke intelligently about the war and the future of Europe and the world, but by dessert his friend had moved onto chess (with the encouragement of his host, no less) and after that there was no stopping him.

'*Although a player's intelligence defines their position, the position limits and guides their thought*,' Estrada declared as the third cup of coffee cooled and the grandfather clock marked the transition to the following day. The latest topic was where the inspiration for moves came from. '*The creator obeys their creation. The player is an instrument of the position of the pieces, to greater or lesser effect.*'

'But the player still comes first,' said Graf who seemed excessively entertained by the radiologist's musings (in fact, she'd rather have been talking about boxing).

'Unless we consider the initial position as one of many and not necessarily the most advantageous for either opponent.'

'*Sometimes I feel that the opening is actually taking the pieces out of their box and putting them in a better position so that the game can begin.*'

'A lovely idea,' Estrada said, smiling in pleasure and taking a mental note so it could be added to his *Philosophy of Chess*. 'But that would be to admit that the position comes beforehand, i.e. the game has already begun by the time we sit down at the table.'

'So, the pieces are alive, in a way, like that chess match at Luna Park,' she said, making an effort to include Yanofsky in the conversation. He took advantage of this to tell them that the show had been so successful that they'd be putting on another performance on Saturday the 16th, this time as a matinée. 'This board alive with light, these pieces are alive with form,' said Martínez Estrada, citing Ezra Pound but Yanofksy wouldn't be distracted and went on to explain that now the idea was to have each piece played by an actual representative of their office. Just that afternoon, he'd been talking to a priest from Lomas de Zamora about playing the bishop. Estrada noted with a smile that in Argentina they were often referred to as *bichos* (bugs) because they got into annoying places. Then, more seriously, he objected that they had in fact originally been elephants. Yanofsky replied grumpily that they couldn't bring elephants into the Luna Park but they could get bishops, knights and worker pawns. He'd even gone to the trouble of finding out which trade was represented by each pawn: he was tracking down actual messengers, policemen, blacksmiths and even doctors to take part. Continuing to show off his knowledge of the subject, Estrada informed him that pawns were in fact initially foot soldiers and the trades idea had been a very late, very Western, quite bourgeois and somewhat literal addition. The blacksmith had been placed in front of the knight, for instance. Still, he liked the image better than the military one because he thought that a chess match was more a reflection of society than an army, and a democratic one at that, in spite of the king.

'Who's going to play the queen?' Sonja asked, volunteering herself with a majestic sweep of the hand.

'A couple of queens of the Mendoza grape harvest, although I'd have preferred one from Buenos Aires, "La Reina de La Plata",' he said, thus ending any hopes of a cameo from the then-young actress Eva Duarte. Sonja took the rebuff maturely (appropriately, given she'd been rebuffed due to her age) and contented herself with the suggestion that they perform the pacifist game from Beckett's *Murphy*. Of her two companions, only Martínez Estrada found this interesting, and he asked her to go into more detail but it soon became apparent that even he was hoping to put the subject to bed. After a brief silence during which Yanosfky prayed that this signalled the end of the evening, he continued with his earlier preoccupation, or reached the point he'd been trying to get to all along:

'Don't you think that the mechanics of the game are in themselves more sexual than warlike? The truth is that

173

chess doesn't represent war, life, or anything else. It rep-
resents chess. But if it is like anything it is the battle of
the sexes, which is more subtle and complicated than war
and requires greater emotion and intelligence. The differ-
ence between white and black is no more than that between
the sexes. Even in friendships, which end in a draw, both
sexes are continuously playing chess against each other,
stringing together different variations, advancing and with-
drawing. And in the game of love, everything ends in mate:
either the woman succumbs and gives herself or the man
is defeated. That is why it necessary to think of chess in
terms of the vicissitudes of coitus.'

A second later, like a player who finds themselves subject to a series of checks with no clear purpose, Yanofsky realized where each and every one of the philosophical speculations his friend had been indulging in since dinner was leading. Phrases that had seemed to be allusions to the game suddenly took on a more sexual sheen. It almost made him blush. The very first idea on the table: '*every chess player is alone and is only ever opposed by some-thing like the echo of their own voice*' (like all good journalists, Yanofsky remembered quotable phrases between inverted commas even when he didn't write them down), which had come out with dessert, couldn't possibly be alluding to Estrada. The suggestion was that the echoing voice belonged to Graf.

In this new light, the erotic subtext to considering the game as a 'reconciliation of contradictions' whose results should 'always involve the collaboration of the losing party', became plain. He also finally understood another of his friend's phrases which previously he'd only noted for its rather simplistic tautology. Ezequiel had suggested that during one of these lonely games (until *the woman succumbs and gives herself* you mean? Yanofsky now thought), '*one does not just search for a good move but strives to eliminate bad ones.*' It was a direct attack on him, Yanofsky because being with him was the bad move Graf had made! Shortly afterward, he'd added that '*a poorly played game can haunt a man for the rest of their life*' and although at the time Estrada's host thought that he was talking about his past as a semi-professional chess player, now he was fairly sure that he was referring to her future in the event that he, Estrada, *the man*, was *defeated (referring*, you understand, *to the vicissitudes of coitus)*. Among the arguments that the King of the Pampas was expounding to subliminally suggest to the Lady of Europa what her best move might be, was what Yanofsky had at the time, during the first coffee, had regarded as one of his friend's typical cognitive digressions when it was in fact a direct attack on him. Although he couldn't remember it entirely, Martínez Estrada was good enough to write it down and add it to the folder that contained the papers he was putting together for an ultimately unfinished book on chess whose fragments would only be published several decades after his death:

> *Given the simplicity of the rules of chess, it seems that the intelligence has found in the game a way to eliminate the difficulties usually presented by the nature of things. Once our doubts about what things are and mean are eliminated, all that remains are our doubts about their possible combinations. One might say that chess has come along to show us that the elimination of the absurd and the complicated, the quest for maximum simplicity, is no more than an intellectual mirage. For the intellect, nothing is*

simple: wherever something simple exists, the intellect complicates it. Perhaps clarifying and simplifying concepts is just a means of addressing the absurdity of the fact that the intellect can only be sure of itself when it is allowed freedom to make complicated mistakes. For as much knowledge as it supposedly possesses, when that chaos is turned to order, when what were supposed to be external difficulties beyond its control are suppressed, when things have been simplified and exist in a pure, original state, one realizes that all they know is that they know nothing. Perhaps, by way of a comparison, the intelligence acts like lungs that need oxygen and seek it out in its purest possible state. But if they ever obtain it, however, they'll be destroyed.

Translating this complex thought to the present situation, *simplifying it*, Yanofsky was the simple option for Sonja: the stupid lover who would smother her in tedium, while Estrada represented what her intellect really wanted; complexity and even mistakes (he thought he was so clever, flirting right under his nose). It wasn't a sports journalist she needed but a pretentious intellectual, someone who said things like '*winning is also a death, it is the end of the game,*' or who could state as coolly as you please that chess is '*a science based not in truth but error*'.

'All the mental work that goes into a game of chess cannot be converted to any other symbolic system, it isn't applicable to a reality and is thus useless,' his brazen guest was now saying, yet another addition to the list of utilitarian symbolism.

'It can't even be applied to sex?' Yanofsky retorted in Spanish so as not to leave any doubt as to at whom the comment had been aimed.

'*Not even if we wanted to*,' said the other man with an ambiguous smile. Switching back to French, he added that the same was true of war. '*Franklin Young reproduced the Battle of Waterloo on a board, but the reproduction of a work of the imagination on a board, giving the pieces and squares conventional values, is far more logical and legitimate than a battle.*'

'Wasn't Alice's story a game of chess?' the woman interjected to the equal amazement of both men, an amazement superseded by their increasingly bitter discord.

'It was, you could reproduce part two, *Alice Through the Looking Glass*, the way one translates a translated book back into its original language,' said Estrada excitedly. 'The idea has to do with the triangulation I suspect exists between the game and reality. *Because if we admit that the game is already a reality, that the game played is an objective work, we can draw a line of experience: from facts to reason and reason to facts.*'

Triangle! Reason! Facts! It was about time to throw the coffee in his face and call him out for a duel then and there. This almost did occur at the Tournament of Nations, as anyone who now chooses to visit the documentary section of the novel located in the basement will soon learn.[9]

---

9 The esteemed Carlos Querencio was assigned by the Argentine Chess Federation to arrange a rematch between Alekhine and Capablanca. He received the unconditional agreement of the Cuban but was met only with intransigence by the Frenchman. He published an open letter to the current champion in *Noticias Gráficas,* urging him to stop shirking his sporting responsibilities and to defend his crown against a rival of his own class. The angry, sarcastic text, as reproduced in Juan Sebastián Morgado's *Argentine Chess: The Crazy Years*, went as follows:

> *For approximately a decade the chess world has been anxious to know the identity of the true world champion. I blame you for keeping it in*

the dark with your conduct and frequent evasions every time Master Capablanca has presented himself. You can't possibly believe that the individual encounters you have played in recent times, against hand-picked adversaries without the authorization of a prestigious institution such as FIDE, have convinced the world that you are a worthy champion. No, Master Alekhine, you're wrong. The chess world is universally aware that you continue to select unremarkable opponents and the pure, unvarnished, irrefutable truth, the one we are all so keen uncover remains denied to us. And yet, you continue to declare yourself the holder of a fictitious position [!] a champion in whom no one believes. You must disavow yourself of this misapprehension and take advantage of the circumstances that have presented themselves now that the two of you are in our country, the country that so generously gave you the opportunity to play that unforgettable match [in 1927] and that today clamours for you again because it believes that Master Capablanca is worthy of the gesture, because it believes it to be one of honour and sincerity, because it wants to know who of the two of you is stronger and finally because it expects that you, out of gratitude, shall acquiesce willingly. And because this is what you promised in front of numerous witnesses of that unforgettable match including the undersigned, a judge for that honourable battle, to whom you said the exact words.

'The only competition I have in the world is Capablanca and I promise you that I shall give him a rematch.'

I appeal, Master, to your excellent memory.

You have argued recently that your adopted country, France, requires you to serve in its ranks [Alekhine did indeed say that now that his country was at war he could be 'mobilized' as 'an official reserve interpreter' and thus couldn't take on any prolonged commitments.] *Fine, Master. I applaud your patriotism but allow me to suggest an elegant solution: PLAY THE MATCH FOR THE BENEFIT OF THE FRENCH RED CROSS. France shall be eternally grateful for your valuable moral and financial support. We, meanwhile, through your worthy intermediary, shall have the eternal satisfaction of having offered our support to the France we so admire. To conclude, we offer our services to help smooth out any difficulties with the Honourable Ambassador of France.*

In his column for the *El Mundo* newspaper, Alekhine answers in amazement at this 'very strange (at the least) way of professing the friendship I feel and have demonstrated so often to this country and its chess family.' Alekhine appears to have completed these thoughts on the newspaper's radio station, which was broadcasting from the Politeama Theatre. In answer, Querencio issued a formal request to two friends (seconds) challenging him to a duel:

> *Following an open letter sent by myself to Alejandro Alekhine that detailed rigorously accurate details recorded in all the annals of world chess, the Master responded inappropriately through the medium of Radio El Mundo, seeking to correct my language in a way that now clearly requires satisfaction. I beg you to present yourselves to this person and demand a documented retraction in writing. Otherwise, you are hereby authorized to begin honour proceedings.*

The mediation took place that night at what is today the Hotel Luxor on Diagonal Norte and the document was published in *Noticias Gráficas*. In summary, the representatives of Messr Querencio stated that during the radio broadcast:

> *. . . Messr Alekhine made use of the word 'crapulous' in reference to Messr Querencio. The representatives of Messr Alekhine stated that the term 'crapulous' which Messr Querencio believed to have been directed at him was not said by the man they were representing in reference to Messr Querencio or the letter that he published.*

Olga Capablanca Clark, the Cuban's second wife, adds an anecdote that makes this duel between chess players look even more similar to one between boxers (esteemed or otherwise). Due to Olga's lack of respect for factual precision (for example, she remembered the tournament as having been played at the Teatro Colón), it ought to be taken with a pinch of salt, but that only serves to enhance its flavour:

> *An amusing thing happened that day. One of Capa's most enthusiastic supporters, Messr Querencio, challenged Alekhine to a duel if he continued to refuse to give Capablanca a rematch. This was followed by bitter words. Alekhine brought the exchange to an end by running to the gentlemen's bathroom, where he locked himself in. Querencio waited at the door, unperturbed.*
>
> *'Come out, crapulent,' Querencio apparently called from outside.*
>
> *'I never said that,' Alekhine apparently answered from inside.*
>
> *'Of course and neither are you going to start writing Nazi lies about how the chess played by Jews is that of an inferior race.'*

But here, in our fictitious (but no less worthy, don't you think?) episode, no coffee was shed. After arguing for a while about the triangular relationship between reality and chess, which led to the relationship between reality and books in the sense that they

---

'*You have no idea what I'll do in the future!*'

'*Why not? Men are like chess pieces: their movements are absolutely predictable.*'

'*I didn't want to write those things. They made me. I was under duress.*'

'*Drunken duress you mean, you worthless drunk.*'

'*Shut up, you crapulent man.*'

'*Did you just say it again?*'

'*You said it first.*'

'*You, sir are a veritable champion of cowardice. Why don't you come out of the bathroom and we'll pit our skills against each other with a pair of pistols in hand? Just think: if I kill you, you'll be saved from the machinations of the Nazis.*'

'*Aha, so now you're doing me a favour.*'

'*Of course. I want you to give Capa a rematch, it's the best for everyone.*'

'*I'll play him later, during the war, if you get me out of Europe and take me to Cuba.*'

'*You see? Now it's you talking about the future. But that wouldn't be later, it would be too late. By then Capa won't give you a rematch. You'll be condemned to an eternal game of repulsed gambits.*'

'*But if you've changed my mind now, why couldn't you do the same for Capa in the future?*'

'*You can't get out of check with another check!*'

You can't put anyone in check if one of the players hasn't moved their pieces!'

I heard that Alekhine stayed in the bathroom for almost an hour, until one of Messr Querencio's friends persuaded him to leave his post. Only then did Alekhine cautiously emerge from the bathroom and escape. The episode aroused much laughter in Buenos Aires. But Capa just shrugged.

contain, in symbolic, *verbal* terms the objects they describe, beginning of course with the book that tells us how it all began, itself included: the Bible, which Estrada brought up to illustrate his latest (also the first, both for him and the world) idea: that the chess move was equivalent to the *logos* of the Ancient Greeks, used to express 'language and reason at the same time', and that the news that God's first move was a verb, the word (translated as *logos*), was equivalent to the idea that in the beginning was the move and only then came the player; or God. As he continued to elaborate on the subject of triangulation, which oscillated dangerously between the theoretical and erotic realms, Yanofksy realized that the one with sex on his mind wasn't his learned friend but him: the official organizer of a public dinner whose only purpose had been to arrange a private match with Sonja Graf. Later, Ezequiel would admit that he'd begun making sexual allusions so that the idea would be in play and thus to help Yanofsky score once the path to goal was left open (all sports metaphors courtesy of Yanofsky). But there was no need to thank him, he hastened to add, he'd never considered chess in sexual terms before; at the most he'd thought of it as a platonic dialogue. He was the one who should be grateful for having been inspired to such philosophical heights by the game.

Not that any of these efforts looked like being successful; Sonja had planned to slip away with the writer when he hurriedly announced his departure. The only thing that kept her there was Yanofksy's offer to play some tango records and, if she liked, to teach her to dance to them. As they moved to the beat of *dos por cuatro*, upright at first and later on the mattress, Sonja couldn't help but reflect that on the board, too, it's almost always the piece that chooses which of the others is going to take it.

16

SHADY DEALINGS

Yanofsky may have triumphed in the race for Sonja Graf's love but Magnus had stumbled upon something for which any journalist would have been happy to pay cold hard cash, or perhaps even affection. The nature of this valuable advantage was related to both the war and the tournament, so before going any further it might be a good idea to provide a brief summary of events so far. Although the first countries to declare war on Germany were France and Great Britain, the only ones to take action and withdraw from the tournament of nations were the British. They did so even before the official announcement by their prime minister, Neville Chamberlain, stating that 'although the tournament was a great responsibility, that created by political events was much greater' and each of them 'had to do their duty'. Thus, we can now affirm without fear of contradiction, the Second World War technically began in Buenos Aires, at least in the sense that it was there that many more countries started to get involved.

Proof that the British statement wasn't a mere excuse is provided by the fact that CHOD Alexander, PS Milner-Barry and Harry Golombek—the first, third and fourth boards—immediately reported to Bletchley Park to join the team of the celebrated cryptographer Alan Turing who, not coincidentally, would later write the first-ever chess program. Working with Turing, our chess players would decode encrypted German telegram messages. In this variation of mail chess against an unwitting (or overly familiar) player, their greatest achievement was to decode the rotating key of the Enigma machine. Some historians believe that this hastened the end of the war to a greater extent than the atomic bomb. 'Not since ancient times, and perhaps not even then, has any war has been fought in which one side has so regularly read the principal reports of the other's military and naval intelligence,' Milner-Barry, one of our heroic code-breakers, would say later. Without wanting to detract from the feat, the only enigma left to unravel is, if that is so, why the hell they didn't win it earlier.

The fact that the British must have been in contact with their secret service and privy to classified information before the official beginning of the war is also confirmed by how quick and unexpected their departure was, taking both the organizers and other participants by surprise. The column written by Alekhine in *El Mundo*, for example, contains the following paragraph about CHOD Alexander who would only have been able to read it aboard the British liner *Alcántara* (commandeered for the war effort): 'The British champion Alexander has thus far been the only sporting disappointment of the tournament [two victories / two defeats / one draw]. All those who know what he is capable of know that, once he is back to his real self, he will make a spectacular comeback in the final round.' And he did, but in the actual war, during which his amiable critic would be on the opposing side.

The apparently fully justified, and perhaps not particularly spontaneous, withdrawal of the British team also resulted in an event of supremely symbolic importance that has nonetheless been overlooked by more reputed historians (leaving it to those of us of ill-repute to make up for their shortcomings, as usual). On the night of Friday, 1st of September, after a rest day for all, the British were supposed to embark on the final and decisive round of the tournament against the Palestinians; i.e. a pair of Poles (Czerniak and Rauch), the German Foerder (later renamed Yosef Porath) and the Lithuanian Kleintstein, all of whom had recently emigrated to the British colony that after the war (we're getting there) would cede its sovereignty to the Israelis. So, one might say, once again rewriting world history through the prism of a game that reproduces and in a way contains it, that the return of Moses' people to the Promised Land was begun symbolically—or playfully, with all the seriousness of play—here in Buenos Aires during the *erev shabat* of the sacred month of *elul*, when the British ceded their four points to the Palestinians.[10]

Now that reality had tangibly influenced the game (while the game, as we are seeing, affected reality in its own way), there was no controlling the fantastical comparisons: the tournament had become a miniature representation of the greater board. *Crítica* was an early leader of these speculations in another of the colourful reports filed by Yanofsky (without ever leaving his office):

A large number of people enter the Politeama to find out what's going on in the game some [Yanofsky] find mysterious and incomprehensible. You hear plenty of speculation about what the Poles will do when they have to play the Germans and in turn what the Germans will do when they

---

10 They would subsequently cede to all the rest as well, with the scheduled matches simply being declared a free day for their intended opponent. But grand allegories pay no heed to minor details. (This footnote is dedicated to Theodor Herzl, *in memoriam*.)

play the French. Imagining absurd situations that will never occur because the chess world is one vast fraternity united by intangible bonds of intelligence, those attracted to the tournament by the sniff of controversy were sorry to find that teams from Italy, Japan, the US and other possible combatants were absent, leaving the stage incomplete.

The 'vast fraternity' comment was of course a cruel irony on the part of Yanofsky. In the official book about the tournament, a brief but eloquent paragraph is dedicated to the issue:

One of the habitués in the broadcaster's stand was the French champion Mr Aristides Grömer. He offered a cultured, talkative, friendly and empathetic voice to listeners of Radio Fénix [which was broadcasting from a studio set up right in the theatre]. *The night after the declaration of war, Grömer was with us. Suddenly Eliskases, the German champion, passed in front of our stand. Their gazes met as though both in askance but ... they did not exchange greetings. Grömer saw in my eyes that I was struggling to stop myself from asking a question and answered it anyway:*

    'We're at war ...'

In the next paragraph, the book goes on to explain that 'due to the situation that had arisen between the teams from Poland, Bohemia-Moravia and Germany', it was agreed that 'the contested points would be divided without playing'. It was an equitable formula the directors of the tournament had come up with to resolve a difficult situation: 'The least bad option ...'

The newspapers were similarly discreet about this peaceful solution to a problem of war. They simply printed the statement put out by the Chess Federation providing information about the 'arbitration' to overcome the 'obstacle' (*El Mundo*) presented by 'well-known European events' (*La Prensa*). A more sensationalist tone was once again struck by *Crítica* which, after reporting the 'highly diplomatic solution', revealed a schism that the other media outlets had decided to omit. It's worth taking a closer look at the complex machinations that went into it, which wouldn't be unworthy of a spy novel.

The scoop was published under the headlines 'Palestine Refused to Face the Nazi Team' and 'They Were About to Quit the Tournament'. In the long accompanying article—written by Yanofsky underneath a box showing how much Lou Nova and Tony Galento were earning for their fight that night in Philadelphia—it explained that the players from the British protectorate had decided to make common cause with the Empire and 'didn't want to face players representing a nation that was currently attacking Poland and responsible for a bloody war ravaging the continent of Europe.' Germany refused to back down and Palestine announced that they wouldn't turn up to that match or the one they still had to play against Argentina so as not to upset the general points table. This alarmed Sweden and Poland, the other finalists, who had already played against Palestine and had higher point tallies. 'The situation deteriorated and there were moments when it seemed as though the entire tournament would end up seeing the withdrawal of the top teams.'

On the urging of the Argentine Grand Master Roberto Grau at a summit meeting between the Palestinian and German teams, the 'conciliatory formula' that had already been adopted for other no-shows was proposed. 'At first the Germans refused to accept this solution, insisting that if the representatives of Palestine didn't play, the tournament regulations stated that all four points should be awarded to them. Finally, after a long, convoluted and fraught negotiation involving many comings and goings and discussions with the German embassy, at the ambassador's suggestion the Nazi team agreed to the formula proposed by Grau, with the serious inconvenience caused by the attitude of Palestine left expressly stated.'

It all sounds quite dramatic and very much fits the style of the newspaper in question, but that was exactly what happened. In fact, the rift was even worse than described. We know this thanks to a private letter from the captain of the German team, the (Austrian) player Albert Becker, which was sent in October and published in January the following year in *Deutsche Schachzeitung*:

My dear friend,

Since I wrote last, the whole world has changed . . .

The onset of war on 1st September caused great upheaval in the chess-playing community. Firstly, the tournament directors asked every team captain if the tournament could go on; the preliminary round had just been completed. All the captains said they would: only the British players Alexander, Thomas and Milner left immediately, so the team was forced to withdraw . . .

You may have read that some of the matches were scored at 2–2 without actually being played (6 in total). The story of how this came about is very interesting. The idea was initially suggested by Messr Alekhine and Messr

Tartakower who didn't want to play in the matches between France and Germany and Poland–Germany (a boycott of Germany on moral grounds). The tournament directors agreed to this plan and communicated it to me. At first I rejected it out of hand, sharing my arguments. They pressured me and started issuing veiled threats: in the end, even the President of the Chess Federation of Argentina, Augusto de Muro, personally visited the German embassy and we gave in on their counsel. Still, we demanded that Bohemia-Moravia be included in the agreement, which they acceded to, much to Alekhine's disgust. He didn't like seeing the Czechs on our side and urged them not to ally themselves with Germany but the Czechs behaved properly and stood firm [. . .] A second incident occurred when the duel between Palestine and Germany loomed. At the time, Germany was at the top of the tournament table along with Argentina and Sweden. Palestine still had to play Germany and Argentina and had already drawn 2–2 with Sweden, Poland and Estonia.

Palestine refused absolutely to play against us. At first they tried the following tactic: I received a letter from the tournament directors informing me that the Palestine–Germany match had been scored at 2–2 and wouldn't have to be played (a fait accompli!) [His parentheses, not ours.] *The explanation: Palestine was a British protectorate, just as Bohemia-Moravia was a German one. I protested vigorously with the following arguments: First, without my consent it is impossible for a struggle* [Kampf] *to be scored at 2–2. Second, Palestine isn't a British protectorate but a mandate! These arguments prevailed. But then came something that we were powerless to do any-thing about. The Jews came with the Argentines to our lodgings and appealed to our spirit of fair play! We were supposed to understand that it was impossible for Jews to play against us not just because Palestine was British but most of all because Jews were persecuted in Germany. They refused to play! To make the idea more palatable, Argentina was also ready to chalk down the match* [Spiel] *as 2–2 without playing so that all those competing for first place would get a 2–2 against Palestine. If not, Palestine 'threatened' to give us four points, in which case any final victory* [Endsieg] *by Germany would have occurred thanks to the goodwill and charity of the Jews. Making it worthless to us! We were left with no option but to agree: 2–2 it was in the matches between Argentina and Palestine and Palestine-Germany. As pure a haggling over points as you can imagine.*

And we still won!

Heil Hitler!

Your faithful friend

A. Becker

The accounts appear to agree, even on the unexpected intervention of the German embassy, but one discrepancy between the two remains to be cleared up: did the Germans try to take the Palestinians' points as *Crítica* says or did the 'threat' (not our inverted commas) come from the Palestinians themselves only to be rejected by the Germans, as Becker claims with a rather threatening cynicism himself?

To clear up the mystery, we must consult a third independent source in addition to the two we already have, one that guarantees true independence, not information gleaned from documents or new research material: one that comes from the realm of fiction. As regards its relation to reality, it's no less unreliable than an unscrupulous newspaper's account (c.f. the Polish bombardment of Berlin before the war had even started) or that of a witness seeking to please his superiors (and thus justify his cowardice in not returning to his country to enlist in the real war). If the two reports extracted from the immediate context can contradict and cancel each other out for lack of a third to settle the question, there is no reason not to recur to fiction, especially in this documentary novel, so that judgement might be passed. In any case, the ultimate judge, the reader (still), will decide.

And so we head to the brand-new synagogue built by the New Israelite Community, or NIC, which was attended by my grandfather, then my parents and finally me. Let's suppose that the Palestinian players were also there on that Saturday. The community chanted the *Shemá Israel* facing the back door (in the direction of the Promised Land, a promise that will soon be kept but at a far higher price than Theodor Herzl could possibly have imagined) to signal the end of the service. It's almost two in the afternoon, stomachs were rumbling. My grandfather had started up a conversation with his namesake Heinz Foerder, aka Yosef Porath, who at the tournament would win the gold medal for second board for his personal record. My grandfather was hoping to share his plan to ensure victory and so invited him to eat at the Confitería Munich (his favourite) but the chess player said that he had to eat with his team at the hotel. Heinz could stop by later for coffee if he liked.

When Heinz headed to the hotel in question for coffee and asked for his new friend at Reception, they assumed that he was part of the chess retinue and pointed him to the salon where the Argentinian, German and Palestinian teams were meeting. And once my grandfather got to the door and saw what was going on, nothing was going to shift him. This was how he came to witness the most dramatic moment in the history of world chess.

'So, we'll go half and half, and then everyone can have their cake and eat it,' Roberto Grau was saying in perfect French.

'There are a lot of culinary metaphors in this country, which certainly makes it a more attractive place to stay,' Moisés Czerniak murmured to Viktor Winz, licking his lips. Winz would later repeat the sentiment to Miguel Najdorf.

'Absolutely not,' Becker said in German. But from the look on his face, they'd have got the message if he was speaking Mandarin.

'Feefty-feefty, as our protectors say,' Winz went on in such heavily accented English that he sounded as though he was a native of some obscure corner of London.

'You're not a protectorate, you're a mandate, Mr Winz,' said Becker, adding a slight noise on to the end of the surname so as to make it sound like 'winzig', or 'little', in German.

Now, Winz just happened to be the shortest man on the Palestinian side and this wasn't the kind of team that might easily have swapped chess for basketball, with the possible exception of the Lithuanian Zelman Kleinstein who was a tall man in spite of the fact that his name contained a German word for 'small' (racial justice, or simple irony? wondered Winz, who regularly thought about the implications of his name). That was one thing. For another, we know that a long time later, when the war was over and he was living in Argentina, on one of Winz' trips to his home town of Berlin to play chess, a man would say to him: 'The air in here stinks, why don't you go back to the gas chamber?' That was in 1960. Two years later, the nostalgic Nazi was given a suspended sentence of three months in prison for his jibe. This pleasant anecdote, which can be confirmed in the newspapers of the time and thus is the kind of truth we call 'irrefutable' (as opposed to those of fiction, which don't feel so pleasant and are thus known as *very-futile*), may have happened 20 years later but has an undeniable bearing on the events in question, in the sense that there is absolutely no way that someone called Winz, someone ready to press charges in such circumstances, would let Becker's admittedly far less denigrating comment pass without comment.

'My surname is Winz,' said he said, a little worried that the man may actually have said 'Witz', or 'joke' which he wouldn't have taken so badly. 'Perhaps you don't know me, which explains your mispronunciation. I, however, am quite familiar with your paternal grandparents.'

Winz was revealing classified information. According to microfiche war documents in the National Archives in Washington DC, in 1941 Dr Albert Becker applied for a post in the Buenos Aires branch of the *Deutsche Akademie*, a body whose purpose was the 'research and preservation of Germanness' (what today we call the Goethe Institute, in the same way that the brain haemorrhage that Grau would suffer in a few years would today be called a stroke). The accompanying correspondence shows that Becker was a '*Mischling 2. Grades*' or second-degree half-caste according to the 1935 laws 'to protect German blood and German honour', meaning that one of his parents was half-Jewish and he himself was 25 per cent Jewish. Hence the rumour (or should we call it a 'second-degree fact'?) that the Austrian Becker agreed to captain the Nazi team in return for being allowed to stay in Argentina and bring his family with him so as not to get into any trouble for the taint in his bloodline. How Winz came by this information, which would only be revealed a couple of years later and at first only to the German authorities—a blatant anachronism on the face of it (even in the future)—we'll never know, but neither does that question interest us particularly because, frankly, it's the truth and one of the prerogatives of the truth is that it has no obligation whatsoever to be probable. What matters is that Becker took it as a threat (the worst thing for a Jew: to be accused of being one by another Jew!) and that only doubled his anti-Semitism (self-hate, the worst kind).

'My grandparents have nothing to do with what is being discussed in this room,' he said, being involuntarily ambiguous.

'I mention them because the distinction is similar to that between a protectorate and mandate,' Winz answered, being deliberately ambiguous.

'Overegging the pudding, one might say,' interjected Isaías Plesci brusquely, who was there to back up Grau.

'Another food metaphor!' Czerniak thought out loud.

'There is no distinction,' Becker replied. 'The mandate [Palestine] is exercised by Great Britain at the request of the League of Nations [the same useless, impotent gaggle of nations that today we call the United Nations], while our protectorate [Austria] is like another province of the country [Germany], or a colony.'

'So you believe that a nation that has been invaded by force has more right to be considered part of the invading nation as opposed to one under the praiseworthy government of another acting with the blessing of a league of the nations of the world,' interrupted Foerder in German, speaking slowly enough for those who didn't know the language to assume that he had offered a very reasonable and detailed counter-argument in marked contrast to that of his opponent. Becker waited a few seconds like a player mulling over an opponent's confounding move, that he initially suspects harbour many hidden dangers but later concludes can only hurt the person who made it.

'Of course that's what I believe,' he said eventually.

'I don't believe that one ought to discuss sovereignty issues with the captain of the team from the country that invaded his country of birth,' Czerniak ventured.

'Especially if those doing so are Palestinians by adoption, as of a few months,' Becker shot back.

'Longer, of course, than the time spent by the Czechoslovaks under the name given them by Germans.'

'Not to mention those forced into exile.'

'Russians are playing for just about anybody these days.'

'I thought that Czechoslovakia was a composite name itself.'

'It's been some time since Olympiads had anything to do with nations.'

'You should have thought of that beforehand.'

'Before organizing Olympiads, or founding nations?'

'In my case, you might say that I was forced to exile myself within my own country.'

'You're asking for our pity?'

'Not at all. And I'll have you know that Austria wasn't invaded, it was annexed. The country had been clamouring to be made part of the German empire for some time.'

'Austrians are separatists with a poor sense of direction.'

'And self-esteem.'

'We asked for a boat full of national pride but it seems that it got lost and arrived in Argentina.'

'Gentlemen, let's try to stick to the topic.'

Grau's admonition served to shut everyone up and bring an end to what might have been a productive digression, if digression is the right word for an issue that encompassed nations and individuals, the game and things that no longer are.

'The core issue is that we're running the risk of this tournament being remembered more for the matches that were cancelled than those played.'

'A competition that lasts in the memory for what we neglected to play, a good metaphor.'

'Metaphor for what?'

'If we don't want this to occur in the future, we should organize chess Olympiads featuring only the countries that existed during the first Olympics.'

'In a continent that hadn't yet been discovered?'

'The Latin Americans could represent Atlantis one, two, three . . .'

'And everyone else Barbarians one, two, three . . .'

'Then it should be played according to the rules in vogue at the time.'

'A philological Olympiad—an excellent idea.'

'You can't tell who's saying what,' my grandfather murmured.

Someone took advantage of a lull to share the anecdote about how Isabel of Castille saved King Ferdinand from losing a game of chess against a commoner after which his Catholic Majesty agreed to make Christopher Columbus an admiral, a decision that saw the man from Genoa head to the other side of the board. So one might say that chess was responsible for the discovery of the Americas. The image brought together hearts and minds and the atmosphere relaxed to such an extent that for a moment everyone appeared to have forgotten why they were there in the first place; there wasn't a single chessboard in sight. The issue that had brought them there was so vast that the only possible digression was into the realm of fantasy.

'Let's get back to reality,' Grau suggested.

'The reality is that, as Jews, we can't play against a country that's persecuting our brethren,' said Foerder (Heinz nodded his head sympathetically from the doorway).

'Reality always plays black,' said Pleci philosophically.

'Let's not confuse things, neither I nor my team is persecuting anyone, this is just a competition [*Kampf*],' said Becker thinking single-mindedly about the game in which the points available against the Palestinians were practically a formality (Poland was another prospect entirely, sharing that match was almost a bonus).

'It is precisely because it isn't a struggle [*Kampf*] that we refuse to participate.'

'That would make a good slogan,' said Pleci, advertisingly.

'And so as to ensure that all those competing for first place remain in the same position, we too shall share our points with

Palestine,' finished Grau. 'Poland and Sweden have already drawn. So the pact is agreed and we're ready to continue the tournament in the same sporting spirit in which it has been played thus far.'

Becker immediately thought of Alekhine, who the week before had refused to face Argentina with the excuse that he hadn't been able to face Germany either for reasons of *force majeur*. Not content with this, in his daily column he had criticized his arch-rival Capablanca for giving the Germans an advantage by not playing against them after playing against their competitors Poland and Argentina. He even suggested that the 'decapitated' Cuban team had lost its other matches deliberately to give Germany all the points. All this under the guise of equality and sporting spirit to distinguish the game from the dark arts of murkier disciplines such as boxing.

'Where is the sporting spirit in M. Alekhine refusing to play with the express intention of harming our team?' Becker said, finally getting it off his chest.

'Dr Alekhine's intention wasn't to harm the German team but to prevent it from receiving an unfair advantage,' Winz replied, turning the argument upside down.

'Still, it's rather odd to affirm that it is in the sporting spirit not to practice the sport,' said the German player Eliskases, who had been forced to borrow clothes from his teammates because his luggage had been lost on the Piriápolis. He hadn't said a word thus far, a raggedly dressed bishop waiting in the corner for just the right moment before pouncing on a piece. It was a judo move: taking advantage of the momentum (and clothes) of a teammate only to complicate the argument.

'Declining to play has always been a legitimate tactic in these kinds of tournament,' Pleci declared, historically.

'I myself have been forced to withdraw a few times because I wasn't in optical condition,' Grau noted.

'Optical?' Pleci chortled.

'I don't understand,' Czerniak complained.

'Say it in French so we can all share in the joke,' Grau said.

'Except for me, I don't speak frog and I'm the one who told it,' Pleci replied.

'But I told the joke,' Grau protested.

'You might have told it, but I saw it.'

'A draw?'

'Not on your life! There wouldn't have been a joke if I hadn't seen it.'

'And certainly not if I hadn't told it.'

'Fine, a draw.'

'What joke? No one laughed.'

'But jocularity was in the air.'

'Like sporting spirit.'

'Do you wish to suggest that Alekhine was joking?'

Now everyone laughed, maybe because the joke had been in a sporting spirit. Now that tensions had eased again, the opponents agreed that the problem with their beloved sport was that it didn't take intentions into account, only the facts. A well-intentioned player could easily move a piece by mistake but the piece would remain moved and there was nothing anyone could do about it. Even when they were allowed to take it back, it cast a shadow that had to paid for by offering a draw at the very least.

Becker made use of this interlude to reflect that if this Winz had so much sporting spirit his team should withdraw and hand over the points instead of seeking a draw away from the table that actually favoured them. If he didn't say anything, it was because he was afraid of being accused of suffering from the same lack of sporting spirit.

Winz, meanwhile, was considering breaking the pact agreed with the Argentinians on the urging of his colleague Czerniak. They could just give the points to the Germans so as to hand them a tainted, dishonourable (in the sporting sense of the term, not the racist one that afflicted Becker, the Nazi Jew) victory. If he didn't say anything either, it was for fear that Becker would agree to be thus humiliated and so risk his own hopes of ranking in the tournament's top ten (Palestine would in fact come ninth).

'We've spoken to the ambassador and he agrees with us,' Grau said, playing his final card.

'This is blackmail!' Becker exclaimed.

'Blackmail by your own ambassador?' Czerniak asked, quite reasonably.

Becker had no choice but to throw in the towel, as they say, although it might be more apt to say that he resigned. By the time the meeting broke up, Heinz was already on his way back home.

17

AN OPEN ANSWER

Here, we find ourselves forced to interrupt the normal development of the novel—a period piece even in its modern aspects—to report an unjustified attack levied at us in an open letter (envelope glue has deteriorated greatly in quality in recent years, unless the issue is a lack of saliva on the part of the sender, although they seem like the kind of person who sprays it around at every opportunity.) In this open, or poorly sealed, letter sent unsigned by someone of scarce phlegm, who is rather too attached to the querulous[11] role assigned by classical phenomenology to the dark side of the book (the reader), in this anonymous letter, the equivalent of what we know today as the anonymous commenteer or troll, the reader who came with us to temple in the last chapter *without a kipá*, maybe because they're goyim, or female, who knows?, chastises us for the profusion of footnotes and quotations, which 'break the rules of the novelistic game'. And yet, he or she or they start out by citing *The* 'epistolary and openly chess-phobic' *Novel of Don Sandalio, Chess Player* by Miguel de Unamuno in which the author of the letters (in Unamuno's novel, not this one) cites one 'Pepe the

---

11 A veiled reference to Carlos Querencio, the author of open letter to Alekhine (note to my English translator, whom I suspect to be behind this devious act / foul move?).

Galician', a translator (ha!) who complains that 'before they used to fill books with words, now they fill them with what they call facts or documents: but what I can't see anywhere are ideas . . .'

Not satisfied with this quotation, the missive moves on to *If On a Winter's Night a Traveller* by Italo Calvino, reminding us that the character of Silas Flannery, a writer, at one point starts to copy out the beginning of *Crime and Punishment*. He copies pages and pages ('he *says* that he copies pages and pages; he's too much of a fraud to *actually copy* them') trying to absorb the 'energy' contained within that great work and thus transfer it to his own. But in our case, our commenteer asks, 'Why on earth are you copying out everything you come across on your narrative journey? Are you trying to teach yourself to play chess?' They go on to ask who gave us permission to reproduce all these accounts, beginning with that of Heinz Magnus. 'It's called *private* for a reason,' they complain. And we, too, would like to know who gave us permission for doing so.

Italo Calvino wrote his anti-novel 40 winters after the tournament of 1939 and in that sense it seems somewhat avant-garde to 'copy his ideas about copying before the fact', the letter grants us. But it is also true, it goes on to admonish us, that several decades have passed since the publication of that important tome, a kind of second Quixote—says Anonymous—'because of the way it teases readers and its powers of suggestion, not now seeking to change the world, but just a few books.' Calvino imitates *Don Quixote*, takes its essence and applies it to a problem of our time ('readers who are rather too receptive; me for one, don't you think?'), while we (or me) would be 'like that idiot who just copies Cervantes, Pierre Menard' (who, by the way, was the guy who 'suggested a form of chess in which one of the rook's pawns was removed'—he doesn't specify if it should be the messenger or the peasant—but after talking it over with himself ends up rejecting his own innovation like someone taking their own piece: that really would have been a revolutionary change!) Calvino also wrote a story about chess—the page goes on to inform us (conveying a message about other pages now reported in this page, like an infinite page boy)—in which pieces serve to represent stories until they end up driving the narrative along and even defining the rules of the story. But where we stop short—the *epistol*ary note fires at us—Calvino goes further and bestows 'a historic fertility' upon the board—the stuff it is made of, the knots and pores of its wood. 'The story is in *The Invisible Cities*, why don't you copy that and show us the ideas it inspires in you for all to see?'

Thus reads our papery interloper. We cite it here, as they must have secretly hoped we would, to show that we fear no form of reproduction of any kind. Quite the contrary. Entire philosophies have been saved from oblivion thanks to the texts that philosophers have copied out just to refute them. A copy is always a copy, but time can elevate it to an original even before the original has disappeared. Something like this happens with Cervantes' quotes from books about knights that no one reads any more, with the exception of those who compose their footnotes (which no one reads either).[12] My grandfather—to compare *casus magna* with the *familia Magnus*—may have been the modest medium by which several newspaper cuttings, and perhaps entire artworks, have been saved. His summaries of the concerts and plays he went to see may not constitute actual copies, but they are the translation onto paper of these ephemeral events. For example, his brief

---

12 Except for a few and only so they can complain later.

report on what appears to have been the debut of someone who would later join the orchestra at the Teatro Colón:

29th May 1938 [Originally in Spanish]

Yesterday I go to the Argentine Institute of the Arts for the first time. And it chanced was the day they first time hold a chamber music concert. I never imagine that such an institute, for enjoy fine singing and music, possible in Buenos Aires. Or that show would be completely free. But what luck, some people interested still in classical music, young people ambitious to achieve high musical quality no matter the reward, just for love of music, love of the idea of a better world.[13] *One highlight is the presentation of young pianist Adolfo Fasoli. Just 17 years old, but looks about 25.*[14] *He play the piano beautifully, admirable*

---

13 My grandfather's faith in cultural output as a means of making a better world is remarkable. The clearest demonstration of his over-enthusiastic humanism can be seen in a comment in his reading log about the pacifist novel *All Quiet on the Western Front* by Erich Maria Remarque: 'If you close a book like this and then find out that it has been read by millions of people, then you can be sure of something: there can never be another war ever again.'

14 Here, held in place over the handwritten text by a pair of extremely rusty paperclips was the first physical document in the diary: that night's programme which includes a photograph of Adolfo Fasoli (another Adolfo!) that backs up my grandfather's description: if it weren't for the Jewish taboo on images, we would gladly reproduce it here so that the reader knows we're telling the truth: both me and my grandfather. But because we have faith in words (even the mendacious ones), we hereby reproduce the paragraph introducing the concert of chamber music, which leaves nothing to the imagination, as they say, because it's nothing but imagination, which may well be its greatest virtue (even for my grandfather, who had to learn Spanish reading this stuff):

If one's soul is elevated on the wings of song to hitherto unknown realms of beauty; if art is the medium of expression of the human spirit;

fingering, understanding of the pieces excellent. It was a wonderful night, my first contact with culture Argentine.

'What's Argentine about this culture, Grandpa?'

'It happens in Argentina?'

'But it's a copy of European culture.'

'An excellent copy.'

'You couldn't imagine it happening in Buenos Aires?'

'First you make fun of me for thinking like a European, then you make fun of my efforts to speak in the vernacular. I'd like to see you writing in German a year after your arrival there. Also, what did you expect me to listen to? Tango? That wasn't music. Look at my entry of 24th July, which I also wrote in Spanish just for your edification:

> *Today, there is other concert with conference about Radio-telephonics and Culture. Dodds[15] explained that no real culture on the radio because tangos and modern jazz songs broadcast called concert. Also, speakers earn so little that only people with no experience, sometimes questionable education, morals, no studies at all, want to be part. So*

---

if the heart bleeds its deepest meaning through music, then how great is the mission of the chamber player in bringing us the subtleties of another time, the emotions of another period, evoking with those songs remote paintings, many-coloured brush strokes, describing emotions that captivate every spirit, from the child to whom it sounds like the song of angels to those whose patriarchal crowns have been turned white by the incessant passage of time.

15 The same guy as the one hawking kidney pills? It's too good not to be true.

education, culture, morals of radio is below what human society have right to expect.

'My goodness. You hated jazz, just like Theodor W. Adorno.'

'Are you saying he copied me?'

'His essay on the subject predates this by two years.'

'Oh, then I copied him without having read it. I don't see anything wrong with that, and neither should you. All culture is copies, transcriptions, quotations.'

'But you don't get anywhere without a little originality.'

'It's enough progress just to preserve what there is, especially in these war-torn times. As a translator, you should know that better than anyone.'

'I still think that your first contact with Argentine culture wasn't a classical music concert but when you went to the Plaza de Mayo.'

'When I came across those people copying European fascism? Still, it's not your fault: I'm the one who got you into this mess.'

18

IN BLACK AND WHITE (OR WHITE AND BLACK)

In the absence of a duel for the title of world champion between Alekhine and Capablanca, a long-delayed rematch that, as we've seen, isn't going to happen here or anywhere else (although we anxiously await the resulting novel): the clash between Vera Menchik de Stevenson and Sonja/Susann Graf was undoubtedly the most popular draw at the tournament. The Englishwoman's reign had never been in such danger: the only opponent close to her calibre was reaching the peak of her capabilities. Until then—the thirteenth round—Menchik had only dropped half a point and Graf a whole one, so a victory for the (free) German would almost certainly mean that for the first time in history the position of number one was held by another woman.

The only thing that counted against the billing of the event was its category. Although they shared the stage, it was as though the men met to play in the living room while the women were forced to improvise games in the kitchen. The worst part was that Graf secretly agreed with this misogynist segregation:

I much prefer playing against men (she writes in *This is How a Woman Plays*, the first book on the subject written by a representative of that gender.) *It seems that they have more interest in the fight, more gusto. Without wanting to hurt the feelings of women, I must honestly confess that, save for rare exceptions, games between women aren't worth much because they generally make moves with no depth, sometimes naively or in some cases remaining rigorously theoretical up to about the fifteenth move. They produce faithful copies of the openings of the masters that subsequently branch off in esoteric ways when their memory fails them. That is why, to some degree, I understand why chess players don't like playing against women and say that there's nothing of interest in their games.*

Although she allowed that men were usually stronger (proving that chess is a sport in the most physical sense of the term, if there are any others), that didn't mean that women couldn't have a 'logical, solid brain'. The lack of professionalism was due to a lack of support for the activity, as though men were afraid to give them proper encouragement in the fear that great players might well arise. The actual tangible differences were manifold: the number of tournaments, teachers, prizes and cash available to each diverged greatly. The sexes were like black and white: convention dictated that one side had the decisive advantage of moving first. Both in the 1937 championship in Semmering (Austria) and the World Cup that year, Menchik had chosen to start her games with the queen's bishop pawn, so Graf had prepared especially carefully for that opening. She did so in view of the Pyramid of May, whose shape and diagonals spreading around it reminded her of an outsized, lifelike bishop. She carried with her the portable set shown in the photo in *La Razón* (the one in which her legs attracted most of the attention) and practiced variations sitting on different benches in the square. It sounds like just another of her eccentricities; she might for instance have chosen the Torre de los Ingleses (don't forget that Menchik played for Britain), which was also in the middle of a lovely park. But Sonja sensed that the bishops would be decisive and wanted the image of the Great Bishop there so that she'd always keep them in mind. And, in fact, by the end of the match, the only important pieces left on the board were bishops. But Graf was wrong about the opening, which turned out to be the queen's pawn. 'The Queen of La Plata!' she found herself thinking (or reproaching herself for not having thought before) while mirroring the move as she had five years before in Rotterdam (when she'd won, but only the first game; she'd lost the subsequent three, and thus the crown, to Menchik). She immediately repulsed the Queen's Gambit, just as she did before but instead of replying to the knight's sally with the bishop's pawn, she chose to move her own on the same side. The fact that the centre of the board wasn't congested with her pawns and that Menchik declined to anticipate her by moving her rook's pawn (the sixth move in that memorable game) allowed her to move the king's bishop to the other side (this attack was known as the Nimzio-India defence) and thus initiate the first direct attack on the king, pinning a knight in front of a pair of pawns. The double castling for the seventh move; or one might say quadruple because it echoed those of Rotterdam, left her in a much more advantageous position than before. 'She's following me, just like in Harrods!' she thought excitedly.

She lit another cigarette with the end of the previous one (why did they make them so short?) The noise in the theatre, which had bothered her previously, was now music to her ears. Not even the shuffling of the audience bothered her. For the first time, she felt a real sense of brotherhood with her fellow players.

'Wherever you look,' she thought, 'you see all kinds of different people gathered together for the same reason, with the same ambition. These players feel at home. Everything else is forgotten! Even politics has been pushed to one side!'

'Everyone experiences their problems and politics in their own way,' she went on while Menchik initiated an exchange of pawns in the middle of the board but without taking it to its logical conclusion, allowing Graf to push one of her little guys (her expression) to the fifth row. 'These players are their own generals, their own dictators. The war begins. Chess is struggle and all struggle is war. Hundreds have gathered together from across the world for this combat, everyone is present and they strive to win, to impose themselves on behalf of their homeland.'

This final thought confused her a little (what homeland was she playing for?) and she focused back on the game, which now reminded her of a battle more than ever, maybe because it never had before and not just in the sense that their respective countries (Menchik's false one, Graf's real one) were really at war. Inspired, perhaps, by these thoughts, she moved her pawns forward en masse, like the artillery regiments of old. Now this was nothing like the game in Semmering in 1934: back then there had been a veritable carnage of major and minor pieces leading to an exchange of queens and an abrupt ending. It wasn't what Sonja would have liked but it was obvious that Vera had learnt her lesson and chosen to take shelter behind a solid wall of soldiers instead of joining her in pitched battle.

During a long wait for the British player to decide upon her move—she turned out to be plotting an exchange of a bishop for a knight followed by a more concerted attack as if she'd only just realized that she was playing white—Graf thought back somewhat nostalgically, as though she were already in the past and only fleetingly restored to the present by means of a book, that if she were to turn around, *wherever she looked in the great hall, she'd see roving eyes lost in consideration of some obscure variation. Odd expressions and players in the most extravagant postures. They'd look comical in anyone other than a chess player.* But they were still funny, and reminded her of other strange images from this and other tournaments, *like that famous player who finds a quiet corner to take a nap while his opponent considers his move. Another who would stand in the middle of the hall with his hands behind his head and remain that way, like a statue, staring sightlessly up at the ceiling.* Then there was the one *who, arms crossed, placed a finger to his lips as though demanding silence of his audience, the one who smoked cigar after cigar, the one who sneezed to refresh his thoughts, the one who never stopped rubbing his hands, the one who paid particular attention to the shadows cast by the pieces on the board, the one who made faces like a clown, the one who drank Salus mate* [subliminal advertising], *the one who talked to himself in mysterious conference with an invisible genie and the one that remained absolutely still for hours and hours.*

Menchik forced an exchange of knights (the only piece involved in the attack following the bishop exchange that apparently marked the end of said attack), and, a little while later, Graf considered exchanging her bishop for another knight but changed her mind at the last minute. They got to move 40 with their ordnance almost unchanged (Graf still had her two bishops while

Menchik had the only knight left on the board) and the game was interrupted until the next day with Vera noting down her next move in a sealed envelope.

'So, you finally came to watch, I was about to get offended,' she chided Heinz, getting up from the table.

'Offended?' the complaint caught Magnus off-guard. Now he really regretted having brought his sister, a great-aunt I never got to meet (or inherit anything from) either. 'I'm very sorry, I was busy going to the cinema.'

Sonja smiled back, caught off-guard in turn. Apparently this was someone so odd that she didn't get his jokes, if that was what that was. She was reassured to see him with a woman, it relieved her of the responsibility, the obligation even, of having to seduce him, or at least to make him like her in the way she needed all men to like her, especially if they were Jews. The relief was complete when her Jewish lover appeared. She chided him for not coming to watch her.

'I was great,' she said.

'You know I take that for granted, not that I could tell either way,' he answered.

Sonja introduced Yanofsky as a special correspondent ('boxing correspondent,' he corrected her, jokingly or otherwise) and my grandfather, who immediately sensed that they were on more intimate terms than they were unconvincingly trying to convey, was especially grateful for having brought his sister, whom he introduced as his girlfriend. Hertha, who'd been wanting to leave for some time and had only stayed because her older brother (not much older, just a year and a half) insisted on watching the match between the fat woman and the tomboy (it may have been the most popular in the hall but that didn't make it any more compelling for the layperson) only now realized that it wasn't the match he was interested in but one of the players. The only thing that bothered her was that he introduced her as Astarte, as though they really were in a relationship and he was sharing a private secret. The prospect of feminine competition (for a moment, she'd thought the woman was his sister) only served as further encouragement for Graf (today she felt that she could beat anyone, even playing simultaneous games). She invited the couple out for a drink.

To avoid the Chantecler, where the atmosphere had turned a little tense recently (Graf herself wasn't immune: there were plenty who regarded her as German), the unequal couples decided to head for Los Galgos on the corner of Callao and Lavalle. Because Sonja was thinking about her last move (she decided that the first thing she'd do the next day would be to force an ending: exchange her bishop for the remaining knight, which was the king's knight even though in one of the quirks of the game Menchik had initially placed it in the queen's knight's starting position. This was the kind of detail that Graf always noticed, not that she knew what good such close attention did her) and the Pyramid of May was still on her mind, the conversation turned to the Obelisk.

'The other day *I was in Lanús*,' said Heinz, meaning 17 July 1938. '*A never-ending journey past a succession of the shabbiest buildings, houses and gardens you can imagine. The avenue along which the bus chugged was fully paved but puddles had formed on the curbs on either side and splashed whenever a car sped by. More than half the houses are in ruins, neglected and dirty, the gardens are rubbish tips, the paths lack cobbles and are impassable. There are abandoned cars scattered around with and without wheels.* I remember,' he went on remembering, or recalling what he'd written. *'That we passed by a vast empty lot with tall reeds and standing water. A swamp! The whole neighbour-hood is as unhygienic as you might imagine. A veritable paradise for disease, flies and germs. And even more so for criminals and thieves. Even our driver could hardly be described as inoffensive-looking. At times the bus seemed to go off-road, it crossed tramlines and train-tracks, plunging into fields of mud and puddles . . .*

Heinz paused to finish his coffee, taking so much time that it seemed as though he'd finished. The rest sipped their Quilmes, bemused as to the point of this story about the area surrounding the brewery where their beer had come from. Only Sonja seemed to sense that it was the precursor to something, a planned move. The image of the Obelisk came to her mind and it turned out to be the very piece that Magnus intended to take, so to speak.

'*And now they're talking about knocking down the Obelisk and building a gigantic monument in its place*!!!' Heinz said, tripling his volume to express his anger at a legislative project pre-sented for consideration the previous year, very soon after the Obelisk was completed. *No government worthy of the name can fail to address these basic social issues: housing, hygiene and the prevention of crime.*

Graf was the only one to appreciate the rhetorical flourish, mostly because she'd anticipated it. She paid tribute by telling him that when she had to plan moves long in advance, she imagined the series as a journey over inhospitable terrain, in her case on board a train from which she observed all the dangers around her.

Heinz nodded firmly and said to himself that because of its griddle-cake design (another food metaphor, Najdorf) the city of Buenos Aires was like a chessboard with a thousand squares (by which he meant a lot of squares but immediately realized that he'd underestimated the number significantly) and that moving along and across it was his favourite game. He told them about the afternoon when he *went with pa to San Isidro, which was an enormous disappointment.* That morning he'd gone to see the *Alsina Bridge,* which *really was worth a look* and the area didn't look anything like the '*hive of criminals*' (he made the air-quotes) he'd been told to watch out for. He also told them about the journey from *Retiro in the locomotive to Florida* [where his future grandson would grow up], from where he continued in a '*Collectivo*' to the river *but as usual couldn't find anywhere suitable for swimming so just watched two fisherman practicing their sport* ('Sport!' Yanofsky scoffed inwardly). Magnus completed his journey around the city with *a long-planned walk* he'd undertaken, also in February, *along the promenade under construction. A large section is already finished but Palermo still lacks its splendid rest area. Then I went to Nueva Chicago and Villa Lugano. The latter is especially remote. There, like everywhere else, one is met with a similar scene: a well-paved road and horrific side streets. There's still a lot to do in Buenos Aires. It will take fifty years for the city to be included in the list of those whose entirety can be visited by tourists.*

'I'm afraid that hasn't come to pass, Grandpa. Tourists don't visit those places today, not even by mistake.'

'It'll take another 50 years.'

'Nothing in this world lasts except for your optimism.'

'I don't know if believing that something is going to happen in half a century is optimism or a veiled form of resignation.'

'Pessimism deferred, one might say.'

'They might. But right now I shall have to defer this pleasant chat. I need to keep working on this filly.'

And that he did, hoping to arrange a date to meet up the following week, Sonja's last in the city (although she'd stay for years). Now Heinz's plan was to take her to the Múnich, his favourite cafe, a programme that again had considerable flaws given that the climate wasn't at all conducive to a riverside stroll and taking a German woman to a German-themed cafe was hardly the best way to take advantage of the exotic setting (you ought to have taken her to see a Nueva Chicago match, Grandpa). Meanwhile, Yanofsky, out of sheer boredom and in spite of the fact that the other woman at the table was a carbon copy of the tiny four-eyes trying to steal his girl right from under his nose (an even match-up, especially in nasal terms), had started to chat to Astarte. Flattered, she eagerly joined the conversation, forgetting that she was supposed to be the girlfriend of the man sitting next to her, not to mention her husband Ludwig.

The temptation to complete the castling (touch move) and have my grandfather leave with Graf while his sister stayed with Yanofsky for 'a jump to the side' (a German term for *tirar una canita al aire*, a Spanish term for letting one's hair down) is great.[16] The exchange of pieces would have pleased everyone, even my great-grandfather given his low opinion of his son in law. And especially Heinz, who awaited the love of his life with the same fervour and faith as that of the Jews for their Messiah. Because

---

16 In that case, Astarte might have been able to tell Yanofsky about the pact that Heinz had witnessed from the hotel lobby, which would in turn explain why *Crítica* was the only media outlet to report on it.

he had no way of knowing that this boon from God would arrive the following year, he might easily have leapt ahead and married the substitute, just as the Christians and Muslims have with their respective saviours. He might not like the comparison, but it's very relevant. Taking the surprise path made available by this book would turn his life upside down, a change just as momentous as switching religions. Sonja Graf was the opposite of what he wanted in a wife, the opposite to the wife he did eventually find (now I'm wondering whether my grandmother wore her hair short at Heinz's suggestion), but if this were the novel that my grandfather never got to write, he'd certainly have indulged himself with a marriage to the chess player and a life of travel and adventure at her side.

Weighing in against this happy fantasy, however, is a looming reality; not only the place where fictional facts must converge in order to become credible (the number one rule of this game), but above all because the material conditions for that fantasy to become real, or at least imagined, depend upon that reality: if my grandfather doesn't meet my grandmother, then my father won't meet my mother and I won't be brought into this world to write the novel in which my grandfather runs off with a gentile (and away from himself) after saving Europe from the war. Or, to put it in my grandfather's terms: the meaning of the novel can't be it never having been written. Perhaps no one will ever find the meaning, or the novel might not have one but what can never be is for the answer to an apparently insoluble question to be the erasure of the conditions under which the question might be asked.

On the other hand, what's the point of writing novels if they just repeat what happened in real life? It would be like two players arguing over a completed game but instead of imagining new alternative moves, just repeating the game as it happened, like sport historians or record keepers. But the fact that one can keep discussing, even decades afterwards, what might have been a better move follows on from the idea that any move that can be imagined is also a move that has been played. Not dissimilarly to sins of thought for good Christians. The board of the imagination is just as real as the other kind because of the curious kind of faith that the game requires. And the same goes for literature. A recorded event has no effect on the moves themselves, it being of no consequence whether they're conceived before or after. Of course, the clock and context lend drama to a game, limiting it to a specific world, that of so-called reality, but the resulting excitement is not a part of the game but life. Life understood as a series of limitations and needs, of little artificial deaths. To see chess in any other way would be like sealing literature the moment it is written, or the moment the book is printed, when that is simply an anecdotal event, not the cause of everything that comes afterward (or what doesn't if the book isn't up to scratch). It isn't a necessary consequence of how we organize time, which demands that we fulfil ephemeral obligations even in atemporal matters.

All of the above casts an unsettling shadow over me and this text I control like a God: if someone, or rather me, writes novels to change my life, or even reality, at least in the sense of making people experience things that differ from recorded events—counterfactual things, they're known as, deriving from the idea of a dispute between counterparts—who can say, I now think, or suddenly see; a thought I hadn't anticipated even though everything is happening right before my eyes, like the moves on the board; who can say, I was saying, that that wasn't what my grandfather did in his texts? Like the newspaper he read with its apocryphal reports of a Polish bombardment of Berlin? How can I tell whether or not the diary is actually a novel? The diary format has been used in novels since at least *Robinson Crusoe* who, as my grandfather himself noted, many thought was a real person and who even today if we didn't celebrate the author as the father of the modern novel, we might continue to believe was an actual victim of a shipwreck.

It's a perfect plan: to escape the life apparently already laid out for him and run off with Sonja, Heinz sat down to write it.

18th February 1940

The diary is coming to an end and I believe that I can write something wonderful and magnificent on its final page. I have met someone with whom I believe I am an excellent fit. Her name is Liselotte Jacoby and she's 17. I am, as they say, in general terms, in love. I have the impression that she is the perfect housewife but also very intelligent and to some degree we complete and complement each other. She is the living embodiment of my hopes for a wife. She is all I can think about, I see her face every moment of every day. Maybe I am not so much in love as someone who's come to the realization that I have found someone who conforms exactly to my wants and ideals. My heart is bursting with joy and prevents me from doing anything else. It would be truly wonderful if this really is what I was looking for. We shall see what the future holds.

Doesn't it seem rather suspicious that all this happens on the last page of the notebook? And isn't it even more suspicious still that far from being the last, the notebook is actually the first of a whole series of sequels that begins with this sudden blooming of love? Grandma Lotti makes an appearance like a Diosa ex machina, marries the poor exile and gives him three children: a picture-book family! He doesn't get to meet, or rather write, his grandchildren but one of them writes him to complete the circle. He is now locked in place next to his false grandfather in the world of fiction.

'You were the god behind the God who begins the plot. I was the mediator for other ideas, not you! You started this absurd dialogue, not me!'

'Of course, I'm your ancestor. If one of us is going to make the first move, the honour traditionally goes to me.'

'And I thought that Czentovic was playing white!'

'You forget that I got to Buenos Aires two years before.'

'So what I thought was your only story, "The Find", was in fact your only factual account, written expressly so that the rest wouldn't seem like fiction?'

'Well, the 50-pfennig coin had been withdrawn from circulation.'

'Does the coin symbolize that Catholic certificate?'

'You catch on quick, don't you? But I bet you don't know that the phrase at the end, *Sich regen bringt segen* really was written on those coins. In German the expression is "Eagerness is a blessing" but Sonja/Susann Graf's translator translated it so literally that it doesn't mean anything. It only begins to make sense when translated as the equivalent phrase in our language: "God helps those who help themselves."'

'So you helped yourself.'

'No, I helped you. I helped you to get me out of the house and into the park.'

'Huh? I'm the girl who appears for half a second at the beginning?'

'And I, appropriately, am the old woman.'

'Male and female as two sides of the same coin, how modern.'

'Don't forget about pawns. Philidor describes them as the soul of chess and that they change sex when they're queened.'

'That operation is precisely what Zweig's oil magnate is advised to avoid in the novel . . .'

'And Czentovic gives Graf the same advice in your novel. But you didn't take Sonja's lesson to heart: "You need to familiarize yourself with the pitfalls so you can avoid them, not use them."'

'Why did you include a girl who could be your granddaughter rather than one who could be your daughter?'

'It's the Magnus effect. Are you familiar with it? It describes the spin that makes balls swerve through the air. Discovered by the physicist Gustav Heinrich Magnus.'

'An actual relative?'

'No, just a spiritual one. It inspired me to perpetuate my fictitious world. If I made the writer your father, it wouldn't have worked—an overly obvious frontal attack, too predictable. I had to skip a generation, put a new spin on the move so it looked as though it was going in one direction only to swerve at the last moment.'

'Well, I fell for it, bamboozled by the spin.'

'I did, but I prefer to think of you swooping in like a knight, because they leap forward and sideways. Magnus explained why projectiles swerve through the air. It was a military problem before it became a sporting one.'

'Like chess!'

'Still catching on! The interesting part was how Magnus demonstrated his effect. Until then, every theory was based on conjecture because you couldn't study a moving bullet. So what our ancestor from another branch [another Zweig] did was to invert the process: instead of making something fly through the air, he had the air fly around a still object.'

'What they call a Copernican twist. Like the one I can see is happening here right now.'

'That's correct, my dear grandson: you're no longer at the centre of your solar system. But this might have its advantages, you know.'

'I'm completely lost. My editor suggested that chess might be a good subject for a novel and my agent had been urging me to write some fiction about my grandfather, so I thought I'd combine the two and upset them both. And as if that weren't enough, my German translator stepped in to reorganize the story so that readers wouldn't lose track. You know how they like to follow the leader [Führer].'

'So it really was written on commission.'

'Yes, but I now realize that the commission came from you.'

'Oh, you were slow there! Silas Flannery, the author-character mentioned in the open letter, who also works on commission, planned to transform his private diary into a novel. You can't say that I didn't leave you any clues!'

'Ah, so the letter from out of nowhere really did come from out of nowhere? Listen, Grandpa. Are they all working for you? Do they know that they're being written or are they just as naive as me? I hope you're paying them at least?'

'In theory, we all work for them but you know that "Theory and rules can't solve all the problems they create," if you'll allow me to cite Sonja again.'

'You read her books more closely than I did!'

'It's as though I translated them!'

'That's it! Now I understand why I've always been fascinated with them. But let me ask you again, because I have what you might call a mother of a question (or rather a grandfather of one): Did you really go to the Adolfo Fasoli concert or just stick the programme in to make the diary seem more real? Was the better world created by music a better world for everyone or just for you? And now that we're on the subject, let me also ask: The fool who "believed that the surface is a reflection of what lies beneath", is that the play you supposedly went to see or does it refer to me because I believed that your diary was a faithful reflection of your life?'

'The fewer questions you ask of God, the better you'll like the answers.'

'Are you saying that because you know him personally or because that's who you are?'

'Listen, my grandson: *man experiences meaning through his relationship with God. The moment that he understands that he was born he sees the hand of the Creator and seeks a connection with him because only when one understands that they live through God can they truly live.*'

'Yes, but *the earth is in the hands of man and his free will, his potential strength. Therein lies his duty, which arises out of life, to apply his earthly wisdom or intuitive nature to reality so that in each and every part of his activity he works towards saintliness.*'

'Looking for God together with someone else, maybe that is the ideal. Within that "together" lies a "through".'

'You've gone right through me when I thought that we were together! That part comparing yourself to Napoleon wasn't conceit, it was humility. As God, you were accepting a demotion.'

'Don't forget that a moment ago you were the one who thought he was God.'

'There was some serious spin and dip on that ball.'

'Yes, the Magnus *de*fect.'

But what I'm really wondering and what it would be unforgivable to leave unresolved is how on earth to put my grandfather (the character) in contact, via Yanofsky, with the living chess priest and have them, with the help of Mirko Czentovic and the anarchists—don't ask me how and please forgive the sloppiness, I'm thinking out loud—make sure that the German team doesn't win the trophy. Not to send a message to war-torn Europe but to dismantle the world created by my grandfather (the author).

I was ready for what started as a game to get out of hand, as they say (maybe it was what I was secretly hoping for) but even in chess I can't plan further than a couple of moves ahead. I like the game to surprise me but I wasn't at all expecting to find out that it didn't ever get out of my hands: it was never in them at all. It's as though the characters were actually being moved by magnets from under the table and me along with them.

I must admit, however, that I did sense some of this the other way around (through the looking glass, Alice) when I visited the bookseller Morgado, the author on whom I have leant for much of my historical data. I told him about my novel and he said that

223

he too had an unpublished book about the chess tournament. As we shared our anecdotes, we came to the Yanofsky brothers and to my amazement he gave me an exclusive look at the newspaper photo showing them together (that's why we don't like images!)

The Argentinian, named Israel, wasn't a journalist, he was a pharmacist. And the hug between the two reunited brothers really happened:

> We *immediately fell into each other's arms*—says the pharmacist in *La Razón* of 17 August, a long time prior to the tournament, so long that I didn't find it in my own research. *Oh, what an extremely happy moment! In a second the fact that we had led separate lives was swept away. From then on, nothing could stop us becoming brothers in the greatest sense of the term.*

I didn't tell Morgado about my Yanofsky because when I thought about it, it explained his reaction, or lack of it, when the two met. Obviously, the young man couldn't have been more surprised: Yanofsky was the second brother to appear out of the blue since he'd been in the country. He must have wanted to ask why they'd sought him out separately. Maybe he was afraid that they didn't get on. The last thing he needed was a family feud to break out the moment he'd discovered his family was much bigger than he thought! How many more children had his father sent to this part of the world? The in-joke must have aroused his suspicion that he was the victim of an out-joke and because there was nothing more to say, he chose to smile and stay quiet in life and in his memoir. And when it came to the colleague from *La Razón* who witnessed the scene and described it in his column of 26th August, he probably didn't even read his own newspaper so was completely unaware of the meeting with the first brother.

But that was nothing compared to my grandfather's need to implement his counterfactual plan, which now turned out to be counter-counterfactual because he had to save Europe and the world from the possibility of *not* going to war. All that death mustn't be reduced to a simple game. Forget your classic endgame puzzles! This *Zeitnot* of a player's miscalculation is of far greater import! To continue with my world and restore the one that my grandfather fictionalized, the first thing that needs to happen is for Sonja Graf to win her match against Vera Menchik de Stevenson and be crowned champion. But how can I prevent Magnus, in another of his well-laid traps, suggesting that if she wins the match, and thus the tournament, it would go down in history as a triumph for the Nazis?

'I'm not playing under a German flag,' said Graf as they were leaving Los Galgos, the couples walking abreast. 'You made the design for the one I'm using!'

'Believe me, history doesn't notice minor details like that,' Heinz said, adjusting Astarte's jacket. 'And neither does the present. The moment you win, the regime will take you in again, just as I read in *Crítica* that they want to do with the Jews, so they can use them as cannon fodder. You can't play the murderers' game.'

These harsh words may have been reasonable but were no less cruel for that. They echoed in Sonja Graf's head right through to the following day when they might well have been responsible for the 'three stupidest moves you can possibly imagine' (the unnecessary, disadvantageous queen exchange of moves 59, 60 and 61 as Alexander Alekhine notes, nonetheless including it in his book

107 Great Chess Battles, the only game played by women to be featured). As Capablanca wrote in *Crítica*:

> *The game continued to be played quite poorly by both parties but especially Ms Stevenson* [Menchik] *who at one point was in such a bad position that it seemed inevitable that she would lose. This was when Ms Graf, possibly exhausted by the great effort* [or a long night] *started to commit foolish mistake after foolish mistake and eventually lost a game that she should have won or at least drawn.*

The match was so iconic that it even earned its own paragraph in the tournament's official review: 'That day,' says the author, 'I saw Sonja Graf cry.'

19
AS TO WHICH OF THE TWO

10th September 1939

Actually, I have nothing to report but sometimes one feels the need to say something, more to express feelings than words or things. My hope is to find someone with whom I can live as good companions. Not as one, but as very good friends. I believe that the sexual aspect is certainly a part of that.

10th September (night)

In fact, I have plenty to report but I was holding it back. To start at the beginning would take too long, so I shall start from the end. This morning I went to Lomas de Zamora to see the priest mentioned to me by the chess (or boxing, or both) correspondent whom I met at the Tournament of Nations (Sonja was playing under my flag!). Lomas de Zamora is a little further on than Lanús, also in the sense that it's beyond the filth and danger. I told him that Buenos Aires would be ready for tourists in 50 years, but I must take that back: it'll be at least a hundred years before it's suitable for its own inhabitants (the tourism may never happen).

I chose a Sunday not just because I don't have to 'laburar' (I learnt the word the other day, and I like it better than 'trabajar';

actually I like everything better than trabajar). I also chose it because I wanted to meet Father Schell while he was on duty. The idea came to me while I was talking to the journalist. I asked him if he knew a priest and when he wanted to know why, I told him that I had to confess. I said that hoping that Sonja would over-hear; I'm trying to convince her that I'm not Jewish. I made the mistake of saying so the first time we met and now I'm doing everything I can to disavow her of the notion. Why, is easy to explain. The motive was the mystery of the cinema being revealed (I didn't mention it in the diary because I didn't want to think about it but it ended up being an advantage as it led to my meeting with the anarchists. They may be useful to my plans). In the mid-dle of the conversation with Sonja, I said something about La Bête Humane *(I know very well what it was: I said that women were the bêtes humanes because of how they make us men suffer) and it came out that she'd never got the message. Her expression when I told her that I'd waited for her outside the cinema was the same as the one at the barber shop in Harrods when she found out that I was Jewish. It was then that I realized that it wasn't affection she felt for me, but pity. Or affection arising out of pity, which is the same, or worse. That's no reason to love me, I said to myself. Then I remembered that I needed a priest and thought to ask the journalist. By the way, I think something's going on between them (because he's Jewish no doubt!).*

And so I came to Lomas de Zamora one Sunday morning. I went to Mass, kneeling and crossing myself when the others did and then I queued up to confess to the priest. I had told the jour-nalist the truth! I realized that if I told the priest my plan during confession (and you might say that given that the plan was to be implemented in Buenos Aires, it was a capital crime), his vow of silence would prevent him from reporting me if he didn't want to help. But to my very pleasant surprise he readily agreed. It was also a relief to learn that although he was German, he wasn't a Nazi but a sensible and even entertaining person. 'I always wondered what the cassock was for. Now I know,' was his curious way of assuring me that I could count on him. The only thing he asked was not to have to shove any legal minors under there so as not to arouse suspicions if we were caught. 'You can explain anything else away, but not that.'

Although we still need to find the diminutive adult, a carpenter to modify some of the tables and to study the fixture list to see which games require our intervention, I feel that now nothing can stop my plan. That is why, when I got home I decided to talk about it openly in my diary. I should have mentioned it much earlier, but am doing so only today! It's a great relief. My pen feels lighter than ever, as though it too were being pulled by magnets under the desk.

12th September

I know who our Turk is going to be! A very strange little man I met on my first trip to the Politeama (or rather didn't, because I never got inside). I couldn't remember his name but I do remember that he introduced himself as one of Stefan Zweig's characters. Only now do I realize that he must be related to Mother, showing once again that we share a family tree with Stefan. I described him to her and she said that he reminded her of a cousin from the Volga.

Tracking him down was easy. He was in the same cafe where I left him. At the same table in fact, sitting next to someone else I met that night, like pieces on the board of an interrupted game. I

229

bought him a coffee and told him about my plan while he moved pieces around on a folding board (what does so much time spent staring at a board do to their view of the world? I watched Sonja's game against the British woman for about an hour and ever since I've seen things moving diagonally or in straight lines, threatening to take other pieces. It reminds me of the first time I saw obscene postcards, a boy at school brought them in and we took turns looking at them in the bathroom. After that, and I admit that I paid them rather more attention than I did to the Torah, I was seeing the naughty images for days afterwards. It was certainly more fun than seeing a chessboard). He was staring so hard at the board that I didn't think he was listening to me but when I finished explaining my plan, he asked what was in it for him.

It was a good question, so I made an effort to persuade him that if all went well he'd go down in history as another Maelzel's Turk, but in a charitable rather than pecuniary way. If we achieved the desired effect, and this looked likely given the tournament's international standing, he might be remembered as the man who saved the world from the greatest catastrophe of all time.

'What I want to know is how much money I'd win,' he said insistently.

I must confess with great shame that my first thought was that he must be Jewish. Because of that and because he was small and intelligent, or at least a good calculator, he was the perfect embodiment of the stereotype promoted by the Nazis. A character like that had been written by Stefan Zweig? For a moment I didn't know who was being more ironic: Czentovic for inventing such an origin, or my favourite writer for inventing such descendants.

I said any old sum, hoping to earn it later from the interviews and talks we'd be giving (like Stefan Zweig!) and we moved onto the details. The journalist had told me that to use the seating area for the tournament they'd had to raise the floor on wooden struts, creating a false bottom that could be used as a hiding place. But I still think the cassock will work better. The problem, in any case, is how to make Czentovic aware of what is happening on the board at any given moment. The coordinates of the pieces can be passed by a code of foot tapping—it seems that inventing the code will be the easiest part—so he'd know what to do in any situation. The problem, he repeated, was the initial position if he was going to be moving from table to table. So we agreed that he should be in place at the beginning of the game, or before they resume after the overnight interruption.

13th September

I dreamt that I was Czentovic and when I hid under the theatre floor I met many others like me. The real tournament was being played in this underworld by dwarves. The tragic part was that I was playing for Germany and I was winning.

14th September

On my days off (it's Rosh Hashaná) I should have set about studying the fixture list but instead I read Emmanuel Lasker (in the periods between headaches, which have got worse recently). Lasker is a Jewish chess player who wrote books of theory. One of these, strangely enough, is entitled Kampf. *Published in 1907, it argues that life is a* majé *or struggle, not just between people but also races and nations. So Lasker analyses how a* macheeide, *a kind of Nietzschean superman who does everything perfectly, should act in both business and war.*

The obvious similarity between the title and Mein Kampf [his struggle] *immediately suggested plagiarism. It also forced me to get over my qualms and read the murderer's book, which meant that first I had to track it down (something that to my very great sorrow, is easier, and even cheaper, than the* Oxford Dictionary). *I flipped through it, paying special attention to the chess metaphors such as when he expresses the hope that the Deutsches Reich 'will play once more on the chessboard of Europe'. There aren't many other boards in the book, as is only to be expected, but what did attract my attention in that regard (with my newly chess-obsessed gaze) was the repetition of the word 'Schacherer' and its derivatives* (schacern, Verschacherung) *to refer to the* Spekulanten, *naturally including all Jews among their number (Lasker mostly uses the examples of businessmen and war to explain how his struggle should be fought). The choice of that word rather than the Latin one can't be a coincidence but must be due to its Hebrew origin (via the Rotwelsch spoken by high-waymen and thieves in Germany). But also, I now think, to its phonetic and even etymological similarities with* Schach; chess. *Flipping through this rubbish, I realized that if it hadn't already been claimed by the meaning 'haggle' or simply 'to steal' (deriving from* Schächer, *or 'thief'), 'schachern' would today mean 'to play chess', as there is no specific verb in German for the pastime. The contrast between the ignoble activity of haggling and the tumul-tuous struggle of the Aryan race reaches its peak towards the end of the worst-read book in history (if we'd read it properly and in time we might not have taken the author so lightly): 'It is no longer princes and their loved ones who haggle* (schachern) *and bargain over the borders of States but the implacable cosmopolitan Jew* (Weltjude) *who struggles* (kämpft) *for dominion over the people. And the only way for the people to rip his hand from the scruff of their necks is at the point of the sword.'*

15th September

Yesterday I happened to witness the moment when the Palestinians refused to play Germany. It seems that this is to the benefit of Poland (and the hosts) but I still thought it was wrong. They should have faced them, even if defeat was inevitable. What good does it do to run away from the Beast? We should have read Lasker better. We could be a warrior race. It's partly my fault for not having set my plan in motion earlier. With Czentovic under the cassock (and Father Schell as the 'one-eyed Jack' as he put it, a great phrase I hadn't heard before), the Palestinians would have had a far better chance and perhaps the prospect of giving the Nazis a hiding would have helped them to get over their scruples. Now, Argentina is in first place with Poland and Germany sharing second and the chance that the tournament might not end up in German hands (I've made peace with the idea that they might not be Polish) has given me pause. There's no point taking the risk if things work out free of outside interference.

Or nearly free: as the special correspondent told Sonja and Sonja told me, the Argentinians are doing everything they can to bribe their remaining opponents. To their penultimate opponents, the Dutch, it seems they even offered women in exchange for all their points. 'They're not even bothering to hide it, not like you!' Sonja said to me.

I was finally able to take her to the Munich. She's still upset about her loss to the British champion and angry at me for having distracted her. Just when she was thinking that that there was nothing harder than winning a game that had already been won, my argument that a victory on her part was a victory for Germany apparently convinced her to subconsciously throw the game. It's very hard, she says, to shrug off one's nationality or race. It was a loaded comment but I was still pretending not to be Jewish and now she seemed to be playing along. I don't know if she's making fun of me or not (like every chess player I know, the only thing I can be sure of is that she likes to play games).

She, too, is going to stay in the country, at least until the international situation calms down, which I don't believe will be happening anytime soon. I told her that my plan might speed things up but if that meant her leaving I'd rather not act on it. For the first time, she looked at me without pity, but there was no real desire in her eyes either. It was a lovely encounter, very intimate. She told me that for many centuries, chess wasn't considered a game of war, but of love. Apparently there's even a medieval story in which a father plays a game of chess against his daughter and because he can't beat her, he feels the urge to take her. She also told me some very private things, including something similar involving her own father (if I understood correctly). After we said goodbye, I wondered whether everything she'd said about chess didn't in fact refer to something else. In any case, my hopes were rekindled. The war has given me more time, similarly to an official game of chess after a certain number of moves, apparently, and I know how to be patient. What I don't understand is how I got from wanting to be a rabbi to pretending not to be Jewish. It's as though exile has belatedly sliced me in two and one of my selves is seeking to take revenge on the Nuremberg laws by marrying a non-Jew. If I find time in my life to write literature, I shall also write the diary of my other self until you can't tell who's Pygmalion and who's Galatea.

17th September

Today, after studying the fixture list and mapping out Schell's moves (Germany have got back to first place and appear to be on course for the title), I met with the anarchists again. I had planned to suggest that they create a distraction if things went wrong. I don't trust them to do any more than that, which is why I didn't go to them beforehand. I was afraid that they'd ruin my plan. And in fact they have ruined it, but for unexpected reasons.

It seems that someone else, working for the other side, got there first. It's been happening for weeks and was even reported on in the newspapers, not Crítica *though (that's not a criticism, mind; since the war began, they've printed the following phrase at the foot of every page: 'Our position is with France, Great Britain and the democratic countries of Europe. Crítica will take an ancient path, there are no grey areas. We support the triumph of civilization and the crushing of dictatorships.' That's my newspaper!). It all began with an incident in San Fernando when a man tried to kill a taxi driver so he could steal his car and wasn't just unsuccessful but, in his rush to get away, left a pair of suitcases in the trunk. The strange part is that the suitcases contained plans and aerial photographs of Buenos Aires, illustrated instructions for building machine guns and handheld bombs and documents about the venom of Argentinian snakes and how to use them as chemical weapons of mass destruction. I didn't believe it, so the anarchists showed me the story in* Noticias Gráficas:

A large part of the texts were in German. There were letters to Berlin requesting gas masks in exchange for plans
of the rioplatense estuary and more correspondence with
different people including one Müller, who is apparently
the head of the Nazi forces in Argentina.

'*Müller is as common a name in Germany as Fernández is
here,*' *I told them quite sceptically, not seeing what any of this had
to do with me.*

'*But it's the same Müller.*'

*They were sure of it because, in his flight from the police, the
man had gone to an anarchist hideout and had told them everything in exchange for protection. Just as the journalists from
Noticias Gráficas had suspected, the young man who shares my
age and origins and apparently even has the same name; he calls
himself Enrique (I told them that his name must be Heinz and
they thanked me as though I'd revealed a secret code) although
his surname is Halblaub, had come to the country a few years ago
and was a Nazi spy. One of his missions, and this is where I came
in, was to disrupt the chess tournament by planting bombs at the
Politeama.*

'*Just like you wanted to do!*' *I said in a tone that might have
been full of scorn, reproach, or simply surprise at the fact that*

violence is something that even the most diverse political positions have in common.

'Just like we wanted to do,' they agreed bluntly without betraying a hint of guilt.

The difference in this case was that the spy was acting on the orders of Goebbels who planned to use the attack as an excuse to expand the war into the Americas. They'd done something similar in Europe: the Polish attack on German positions that Hitler used as an excuse to justify the 'counterattack' had in fact been carried out by the Germans themselves, as my namesake Halblaub revealed. They'd chosen the Tournament of Nations to repeat the strategy because it was the closest thing to total war on the continent. The Nazis planned to blame the attack on the Russians (thus explaining why they hadn't come) so that the Americans (who also hadn't come) would join the war against Communism, which they saw as the only true enemy on the continent.

'But they've just signed an agreement with Russia!' I protested.

'Only to gain time, according to Halblaub,' they said and I secretly hoped that they were right, although I said nothing.

Whatever the truth of the matter, once the mother of all battles was over, the plan was for Germany to take over Europe and the US to conquer Latin America.

Everything they said sounded like nonsense, whether it actually came from the supposed spy or they'd made it up themselves. But it showed me that an attack, violent or indirect, would only be to the detriment of the interests we sought to defend. Even the anarchists had come to the same conclusion and no longer wanted any part of it.

'The other war started with a terrorist attack, you can't end this one the same way,' they informed me, much to my amazement.

In fact, now they wanted the German team to win because this Heinz Halblaub had told them that there were Austrians of impure blood on it who weren't even planning to go home afterwards. Winning with the help of Jews was humiliation enough.

I left them plotting their never-ending conspiracies and went home very slowly, quite depressed. I thought about Sonja letting her opponent win for a lost cause and now I was the one who pitied her deeply. And myself. All that long-sought-after excitement suddenly fizzled into nothing. Now it seemed like one big joke.

20

HERE ENDS THE PLOT

In the end, everything happened as it should and the German team won, although its members did indeed stay on this side of the ocean, some until their deaths. You could write another book researching how much influence secret groups had on that triumph: there must be a reason it has never since been repeated.

The death of Vera Menchik de Stevenson in a German bombing raid might also be chalked up as a Nazi victory although with weapons more befitting the terrifying Wehrschach than 'the most noble and spiritual of games'.[17] The endemically politically incorrect Sonia Graf was quick to declare herself champion of the world by default. And before moving to the United States, in a truly macabre twist, she married the merchant sailor Vernon Stevenson and took his last name.

For Ilmar Raud, who died in poverty on the chess-board streets of Buenos Aires, Noah's Arc, an arc of several

---

17 Nazi chess, based on a '121-square board' with pieces in the shape of 'war planes, tanks, infantry soldiers and (. . .) V2 rockets' as described in the third chapter of *Chess with my Grandfather*, of disputed authorship.

Noahs given that each team captain fulfilled the divine command of saving examples of their national species from the flood (two pairs each!), on which he had lived side by side with chess animals of both sexes, turned out to be a trap, just like when a bishop is trapped behind its own pawns. The only player among those who stayed in the country to meet a similarly sorry fate was the Lithuanian Movsas Feigins.

Some headed for the interior of the country and one of them, who stood out in his homeland for his raw chess-playing talent but was otherwise poorly educated and didn't know Spanish, went north to the Paraguayan Chaco, where he was told that the pay was better. He suffered through a terrible ordeal! In the depths of the jungle, he was attacked by a panther and only survived by a miracle. He was better off dead! Almost immediately after he lost his documents, or they were stolen, and he became a pariah, someone without a homeland. Disappointed with his Chaco adventure, he tried to return to Buenos Aires but they wouldn't let him back into Argentina. He went from one mate plantation to another, then moved on to the cotton and tobacco fields. He did a little of everything and even became a docker and smuggler. He eventually managed to get back to Buenos Aires. You see him every now and again, looking ghostly and poorly dressed at the chess rendezvous of Buenos Aires.

And getting back to the hero of the novel, everything happened as it was supposed to for him too. He met his 'Lotti' in January 1941, they married the following year and his three children duly followed.

In 1966, Heinz Magnus suffered a severe heart attack.

Ironically, what saved him was failing to follow the instructions of a certain cardiologist with a murky ideological past. 'If you had taken the Cenestal, you wouldn't have lived to tell the tale,' his GP told him (unaware that Magnus had in fact written one). Ten years later, as he was sitting with his son in a hospital waiting room, he read an interview with the Dutch player Lodewijk Prins in a Dutch magazine in which the player revealed the Argentinians' attempts at bribery. He was about to remark to his son about how strange it was that they had a Dutch magazine there, not to mention the fact that he could read it (he didn't know Dutch) when he was informed of the birth of his first male grandchild (Ariel).

After learning of his heir's precocious literary inclinations, he would tell him about how he asked Monsignor Schell to certify that he was Catholic so that he could take the piece of paper with him on a trip to the US, which he embarked upon to visit his impossible love Susann 'Sonja' Graf de Stevenson. 'It's the novel I never wrote,' he told him, 'I leave it in your hands.'

The grandfather died at the age of 72 as he was walking through the park. His grandson would never be able to explain why the Catholic certificate was dated after the trip to the United States. Neither would he look into it much: he never became a writer of novels, 'those elaborate frivolities'.

Mirko Czentovic, December 2015